Connections 5   I NEED A WORD

Published by Lulu for www.connectior

CW01496161

This edition first published in Novem__. ____

ISBN: 978-1-326-44473-0

Rosemary

Thanks for your support

ALSO BY PAUL STUART

Connections - Who Did You Sit Next To Today? (Paperback)
Connections 2 - Hell Has No Fury
(Paperback)
Connections 3 - That's None of Your Business (Paperback)
Connections 4 - Which Room Did You Stay In? (Paperback)
The Mobile and the Ring - The John Lomax Story (Paperback)
The Mobile and the Ring - The John Lomax Story (Hardcover)
Lomax and the Biker - The Trilogy
(Hardcover)

ACKNOWLEDGEMENTS

This book has taken me longer to write than any of my earlier efforts. For the first time since I began writing there were periods when I couldn't move it forward. When asked, I made the excuse that I am only going to produce one per year from now on. Looking back, that's what it was: an excuse. Thankfully, there were many who kept asking and I am grateful to them for their encouragement and gentle badgering.

My wife has, as with all the previous novels, supported me throughout. She constantly reads and re-reads material and makes suggestions, offers opinions and guides me along the way. There was one real sticking point in this novel, and she was clever enough to identify the problem. What would I do without her?

I would like to thank my parents for their continuing support. Tiffany at Radio Cornwall? I'm still waiting for her to decide which part she wants in my previous novel. Thanks also to all my friends at St Piran's in Perranarworthal and to everybody who buys my books. I don't know all of you, but, please, keep it up!
Paul

PROLOGUE

He recalled the woman he had murdered on his way to meet Lisa Richards. She had felt very little as he slipped his thin cord over her head from behind and pulled it into a noose. He tightened the garrote by turning the screwdriver that he had looped through it. A few turns later and she had ceased struggling; her body limp. He had not even broken sweat. He listened carefully and checked the front of the house through the window. All was quiet and undisturbed. He lifted his sleeve to look at his watch and was more than disappointed to note the time. He would not be able to complete his task and made a mental note to himself to plan more carefully next time.

He slipped out of the house, walked back down the drive and settled himself into his car. He removed the latex gloves and wondered whether the tipsy woman had even noticed them. As he started the engine he brought to the front of his mind the name he had given for the evening appointment. Quentin Legard.

Remember that name.

At the White Horse Inn Lisa Richards was confused. She had succeeded in getting over her husband's infidelity and had planned his demise. The man sitting next to her had been hired to do the job and had proved most proficient. Her confusion was caused by his unexpected appearance at the Inn and then his involvement in the events of the last few days. It seemed he had another side to his character; a softer, more human side.

She did not know his history and could not possibly have been more mistaken. She certainly didn't know that he was no stranger to Exmoor. Equally as significant was her ignorance of the fact that he was at that moment remembering the dark days of his earlier life. The awful, terrifying days of being bullied at school, the loss of his parents at a tender age, the lack of love. Every facet of his formative years had joined forces to leave a deep and lasting legacy. He had grown into a man with a particular view about his fellow human beings and the most powerful force that influenced his every act was a desire for revenge. It controlled him, and in his experience it was a dish best served cold.

He sat beside her now with a peaceful smile on his face, and her hand in his on his thigh. He had become impervious to the noisy buzz around him as he focused on his own history. He remembered particular events and people; the darkness; all the most important ingredients that comprised his formative years. The days that had helped make him the genius he now considered himself to be.

THE BULLYING

-1-

He felt the pressure of growing up. From as far back as he could remember, people always expected things from him. He never understood why, but it seemed that more was expected from him than his peers or, as far as he could ascertain, anybody else he knew. He remembered starting school, at about the age of four or five. Children were expected to have an afternoon nap and he could never understand why. He wasn't tired, so why should he sleep? With one of his bursts of adult insight, he thought it was more likely that the teachers wanted some down time. He never slept. He merely pretended with his eyes closed, listening intently to the voices around him, gathering information. He was collecting and storing for future use. He was learning even at that tender, nascent age.

The other children saw him as odd. He was too quiet for their liking and he didn't join in. What normal boy did so much reading? They thought he had 'issues', although they did not use those terms. He could answer any question the teachers put, and his classmates resented him for that. It was, then, natural that he became the target of their attentions.

On one occasion, two older boys, Jake and Barry, who had left the school during the summer term and had therefore started at the local 'big school', suddenly appeared early one morning. They had heard that there was a new boy, and they had decided to demonstrate the natural order of things in the locality. A training day at their own school provided the perfect opportunity to pay a visit. They had arrived early so that the teachers had not themselves arrived. Young children were gradually filling the playground and forming groups, laughing and playing together. Quentin Legard was easily identifiable because he was standing apart from the other children. Notwithstanding that Quentin was much younger than themselves and he therefore had no chance of mounting an effective defence, they had beaten him badly before a teacher appeared and put a stop to the demonstration. Quentin had uttered not a word or a moan during the ordeal. He had merely soaked it up and stored it, like a sponge. Their day of reckoning was to come sometime later.

His mind then turned to a time when he was suffering at the hands of a fellow pupil, every day. It involved bruises and cuts most break times and lunch hours. Again, Quentin soaked it up and stored it. His answer was to wait for the boy concerned to appear round the corner, running at a great rate of knots, only to meet, at full tilt, Quentin's clenched fist. As the boy lay groaning, Quentin stamped on his hand. The overall result was plenty of blood and a broken nose and finger.

Early in his time at 'big school' his jumper had been torn by a boy older than him. He was very upset because he knew how hard it had been for him to be provided with the correct uniform, so that he was just like everybody else and didn't stand out. That boy's name was Jake and, as usual, Quentin had soaked it up and stored it.

Teachers were just as bad. He winced at the recollection of the French teacher who couldn't control the class. Chaos was the order of the day whenever French was on the timetable. That teacher had a bad temper and regularly aimed the wooden backed board rubber with unerring and painful accuracy at any poor soul who couldn't decline a verb. Quentin's answer was to entertain his classmates by hurling a heavy wooden desk through the classroom plate glass window from two storeys up. It smashed into a thousand pieces on the tarmac playground below, narrowly missing several children. Then there was the Maths teacher. Legend had it that he was a Welsh boxing champion and he used this myth to advantage. He was in the habit of applying his hard knuckles to a boy's head with considerable force, whilst demanding that he come up with the answer to whatever difficult question he was asking. Needless to say the poor young victim couldn't think because his head was ringing. Quentin never did exact any revenge upon him. He merely soaked it up and stored it. You cannot win every battle.

He was lost in his memories. He could go on forever, but of one thing he was certain. You can solve some problems immediately, but there are others which need more carefully planned retribution. His mind turned to some examples.

-2-

"I'd help you if I could," the boy said, "but I can't."

"Can't?" Barry mused, peering down at him. "Can't or won't?"

"I really believe he knows something," his partner Jake said.

"I absolutely agree," Barry added, letting his fingers play across the police riot baton which gleamed black and menacing.

"We can't do anything now," Jake sighed. "Come on."

It was August on Exmoor and the river which bore its name rolled lazily by, doing nothing to take the edge off the heat. The temperature had been at a record high all year and as the summer wore on the intensity increased day by day. Normally placid people struggled and there were regular disturbances across the area as people lost tempers that were usually controlled. In local towns arguments over such trivial matters as queuing for ice creams broke out, whilst across Exmoor horse riders, drivers, visitors, farmers and cyclists clashed almost daily, but couldn't define what their differences actually were. Throughout the country the population was irritable, on edge, and not even the occasional late evening thunderstorm and lightning display could calm them.

But tonight was different. The two young policemen had been pulled from their own dozing stupors by an armed robbery. Such an event had been almost unheard of in that part of the world since the legendary days of Faggus and other highwaymen.

In many ways the method used in the current incident bore striking similarities to the method used in those days, because this was nothing less than a highway robbery, albeit the vehicle was an armoured car. It was the same as stopping a stagecoach and had apparently been equally as easy. Neither policemen could recall such an event in their admittedly brief time in uniform, but both were secretly excited that it had happened on their patch. The imminent arrival of a variety of higher ranked uniformed officers and plain clothes detectives did not, however, fill them with great joy and comfort. They were convinced they could solve the case quickly and easily. Moreover, they had already made an arrest, and he was languishing in one of their cells. They had a suspect and, here in front of them they had an eyewitness, reluctant though he undoubtedly was.

Jake sat down across from Quentin Legard. He was in his early twenties and only three years younger than the policemen themselves. Their paths had crossed at school. At that time Quentin Legard had been as thin as a rake and even then his eyes were as sunken as those of any serial killer.

"Now, Quentin," Jake said as kindly as he could, "we know you saw something."

"Come on," Legard answered, his fingers drumming uneasily on his bony knee. "I didn't. Really."

Barry, who was breathless and sweaty, partly due to the heat and partly as a result of his obesity, took over when his partner glanced at him.

"Quentin; that just doesn't gel with what we know. You sit in your garden and spend hours and hours and hours doing nothing except watching the river." He paused and wiped his forehead. "Why do you do that?" he asked curiously.

"I don't know," replied Legard, even though everybody in the area knew the answer.

When Legard was much younger his father had drowned, and he spent all day, every day, gazing out at the river that had claimed him. It was rumoured that he read strange books and unsavoury magazines whilst listening to 'sick' music, which he played far too loudly in the opinion of those around his home. After his father's death an 'uncle' had come to stay. His mother explained that she needed his help to make ends meet and to provide her son with a male presence. She had recognised from an early stage that he was different and she convinced herself that the boy needed a man in the house. Quentin was never convinced and was resentful of this new man in his life. He never accepted him, in spite of his mother's entreaties.

The locals had formed firm opinions about him as well. He'd seen the boy through his education and at the age of eighteen Quentin had gone to college. Four years later Jake and Barry had been surprised when Quentin returned in the June. He lost no time in removing his 'uncle' from residence. Nobody knew why his 'uncle' vacated the house almost as soon as Quentin came back, and only Quentin knew the circumstances of his departure. As far as the rest of the local community were concerned, the man had gone back to his wife many miles away when Quentin returned from College. In fact many were pleased to see the back of him as he had never made any effort to integrate. The fact that Quentin's mother departed with him surprised nobody.

He took to living by himself in the dark, lonely house overlooking the river. In that place, where the gorse and heather did battle with the sou'westerlies, loneliness seeped into his very soul and his destiny was decided. People assumed he survived on his deceased father's savings and were curious as to how he lived so comfortably as to not have to work. They had no way of knowing that his father had left everything to him in his will, specifying in particular that his mother received nothing.

The two policemen hadn't liked Quentin at school. The way he dressed, the way he walked, the way he didn't comb his hair, the way he talked to the others in what they considered to be a sick whisper. They took particular exception to the way he talked to girls, which was not healthy; not joking or gossiping, but just talking softly in a manner that seemed to hypnotise them. He was in the chess club and the computer club and didn't take part in any sport or team activities whatsoever. He was always able to give the correct answer to the teacher in any subject. Nobody likes a loner and a clever one was even worse, so he was inevitably picked on. Everybody sniggered at him behind his back, but stopped immediately whenever his scary eyes alighted upon them.

Now he was back and it wasn't right, just sitting there reading. Jake was certain it was porn and Barry was also convinced the music was satanic. It was all simply unnatural. Every time reports of any crime to them, they immediately thought of Quentin Legard. Try as they might, and they had many times, they had never been able to connect anything to him. They knew he disappeared for long periods of time and were pretty sure he'd vanish onto the moor and peer into girls' bedroom windows. They convinced themselves he was a voyeur; he had a telescope next to his mother's old chair and they thought that was sufficient proof. He was simply odd, weird.

So Jake and Barry never missed an opportunity to hound him, just as they had done at school. They constantly sat outside his house in their marked car, believing their presence would unsettle him. They stopped and searched him at every opportunity. They even monitored his mail and phone despite having no official clearance. Quentin Legard never reacted. He just kept himself to himself, living what they considered to be a shameful life. They didn't appear to have any effect on him at all, which annoyed them intensely, so they were pleased with themselves that they had him, trapped in the interview room, apparently frightened, twitchy and sweating in the summer heat.

"He must have walked past you," Barry stated in his grumbling voice. "You must have seen him."

Quentin noted to himself that these were two statements rather than questions and therefore didn't strictly require an answer, but he decided to be helpful anyway.

"No, I didn't."

He kept it short. No need to be that helpful.

The man they were talking about was Derek Bell, presently sitting unshaven and stinking in a nearby cell. He was scruffy, early middle aged and was always in trouble with the law. He'd never been convicted of anything apart from wasting police time and reasonably frequent spells in custody sleeping off the effects of alcohol and being released in the morning each time with nothing more than a warning and a headache. The local police knew he was behind a number of petty crimes that occasionally bedeviled the area and he'd been picked up as rapidly as possible after the robbery. They thought it was out of his league, but could not be sure. Besides, they had no other possibilities, so he became the leading suspect. He had no alibi for the time of the crime and, although the armoured car's driver hadn't seen his face due to the ski mask, the robber had carried a baseball bat and a bat of that type had recently been purchased in that area. There had also been reports of the theft of a particular type of explosives from a quarry elsewhere in the county which matched that used in the robbery.

They had found him in the early evening, sweating and acting guilty, walking along a main road, even though he had a perfectly good car at home. He said it was playing up, but it had fired first time when Barry tried it later that evening. Bell had also been in possession of a hunting knife. When asked why he just said, "well, I just, you know, am."

Barry and Jake had never read any training manuals but they recognised motive, means and opportunity when they saw them. In their eyes it was simple. There was no doubt in their minds that Bell had carried out the crime and because Quentin Legard's house was in a direct line from the robbery to where they had found Bell, there was no doubt that he could be placed near the scene of the crime.

"Just tell us you saw him," Barry sighed.

"I can't, because I didn't," Legard answered, again noting the lack of a question.

"Look Quentin," Barry continued as if talking to a five year old child, "you understand how serious this is. Bell smashed the driver over the head with a baseball bat. He's in a coma."

"Oh, is he going to be Ok?" asked Quentin, soft and untroubled.

"Don't interrupt me!" shouted Barry, beads of perspiration running down inside his shirt. "We know Derek Bell. We know what he's like, what he's capable of. You mustn't think you can just keep quiet and everything will be alright. It won't. That's not how it'll work. You should be afraid."

Another statement. Quentin Legard realised he hadn't been asked a single question. In fact he was the only person to have posed a question. He asked another.

"Why should I be afraid?"

Barry almost lost control. He clenched his fists and ground his teeth. "He'll come for you with the bat and his knife and you won't stand a chance. Not a prayer," he shouted.

"If you don't tell us about him now," Jake offered, "how long do you think it will be before he finds you?"

Legard smiled inwardly at the first direct question and the recognition of the good cop, bad cop routine.

"You mean because he thinks I'm a witness?" queried Quentin.

"Exactly!" roared Barry, "and I won't give a damn. You'll deserve every last ounce of pain."

"Go easy," said Jake, playing his role. "Look Quentin, tell us you saw him and he'll go away for twenty or thirty years. You'll be safe, so you can continue with whatever it is you do with your life."

"I want to do the right thing," Quentin said, "I really do." He scrunched his eyes closed, apparently thinking hard. "But I can't lie. I can't. My father; you remember him, he taught me never to lie."

Barry plucked his shirt away from his body and examined the patches of sweat under his arms. He walked in a slow circle around Quentin.

Finally Jake said, in an easy voice, "Quentin, you know we've had our disputes."

"I know you picked on me at school," Legard put in.

"Oh, that was just playing around," said Jake. "We didn't mean anything. We only did it with the people we liked. A sort of recognition. A compliment really. I admit it got a bit out of hand sometimes, but let's let bygones be bygones. We're adults now. We need to deal with this. I apologise for anything that upset you," he said holding out his hand to be shaken.

"I'll second that," added Barry, shooting out his paw as well. "Now Quentin, man to man, what can you tell us?"

"Well, I did see somebody, but I couldn't swear it was Derek."

Jake and Barry exchanged glances. Both were surprised as Quentin carried on quickly.

"I'll tell you what I saw."

Jake, who had the worse handwriting of the two but could spell better, flipped open his notebook and began to write.

"I was sitting in my garden reading..." Legard began.

"Porn, I bet," sniggered Barry.

Quentin ignored the interruption. "And listening to music."

Barry sniggered again and Jake shot him a warning glance, before returning to Legard and smiling his encouragement.

"I heard a car. I remember because it had a noisy exhaust. Then I saw somebody running across the moor on the other side of the river. He was carrying some bags. Then he just disappeared. I don't know where he went; I really don't know that part of the moor very well."

Both Barry and Jake knew that to be a lie. Quentin Legard knew it like the back of his own hand.

"Can you give us a description?" Jake asked, continuing with his role as 'good cop.'

"I'm sorry," Legard whined deliberately. "I'd help you if I could, but I just couldn't see."

"That's alright," Jake concluded, "you've been a great help. We need to check a few things, so I think it would be best if you stayed here for now."

"I need to get home," Quentin objected. "I've got things to do."

"I bet you have," Barry replied before he could stop himself.

"We'll be back as soon as we can," Jake smiled as the two policemen left the room.

"Wait," called Quentin Legard, "can Bell get out?"

"No, it would be almost impossible for him to escape."

"Almost?" Legard queried.

He received no response because the room was empty and the door closed before he had even spoken.

-3-

They walked to their marked car and swept out onto the road. They talked as the scenery swept hurriedly by and decided that Quentin had made the most of what he had told them so that he could get home. They were therefore surprised when they spotted fresh tyre tracks in the failing evening light. They followed the trail and, quietly, leaving their car, came up on either side of the newly found vehicle.

"Hasn't been here long," Barry said, laying the palm of his hand on the warm bonnet.

Jake spotted the keys in the ignition and turned the engine over. The result was a roar from the exhaust pipe and he hurriedly switched it off lest it should be heard. The car was searched, but they found nothing until they came to the boot. Jake lifted out a large security cash bag, labelled with the very logo of the company which had suffered the robbery. He opened it and pulled out thick wads of notes. With bulging eyes they counted and arrived at a total of fifty thousand pounds.

"That's more than my annual salary," said Barry.

"And mine," added his colleague.

"Now where's the rest?" Barry pondered, his mind crowded with possibilities.

"Which way's the river?"

"There. Over there."

On foot, they started through the vegetation that bordered the Exe, searching for footprints or any sign at all. They found none.

"We can look again in the morning. Let's try closer to his house while we've still got some light," suggested Jake. They could see Quentin Legard's house from the water's edge. They scoured the vicinity and identified several possible hiding places, including one that seemed to be a small hollow behind a waterfall. Barry lost the imaginary toss and dropped to his hands and knees. In an instant he had disappeared from view completely and was breathing hot, murky air. It was not a pleasant place to be and Barry was not comfortable in enclosed places.

Jake waited for his friend to re-appear for what seemed an age. Worried, he eventually bent down and called "you ok?"

He had to dodge another canvas bag as it came flying out of the mouth of the darkness. He recognised the flash of a familiar company logo as it passed his head.

"Hey" Watch out you idiot!" yelled Jake in alarm.

Barry emerged grinning from ear to ear, determined not to let his fear show. "Sorry about that. Now let's have a look, shall we?"

They began counting and didn't stop until the final note had been ceremonially placed on the pile and the total had reached eighty thousand pounds.

"It's the only one in there," said Barry. He didn't know that with any degree of certainty, but was definitely not going back to make sure. "Derek Bell must have put the bags in different places."

"Why would he do that?" Jake queried.

"He was trying to put people off the scent," explained Barry.

"Shit for brains," replied Jake, as he began to search the immediate area for any more likely hiding places.

After a long but not very thorough search, and feeling hot and itchy with sweat, they concluded that there was nothing more to be found. They looked down at the bag. Neither said a word. Jake glanced up at the sky, which was clear and glowing with brilliance and promise. They stood on either side of the canvas bag like nervous teenagers and rocked on their heels. The moor beneath their feet was black and soft, exuding menace in the silver moonlight, as if it was about to swallow them whole. In different circumstances each had walked on the moor with a teenage lover, looking for a place to lay. There had been no brooding menace then.

Jake broke the silence. "Barry, this is a lot of money." He knew he had stated the obvious, but could think of nothing else to say.

"Hmm," was all Barry could offer as his mind raced.

"Well?" said Jake, becoming uncomfortable.

"There's a lot of money," said Barry, echoing his companion's words.

"Don't beat around the bush," Jake hissed, afraid they could be overheard.

"I'm thinking," Barry whispered. "We're the only two people who know about this."

"Now who's got shit for brains?" exclaimed Jake. "What about Legard and Bell?"

Barry tried to think, but was finding it increasingly difficult as the life changing sum gnawed at him, working its insidious magic. Finally, he said, "what would happen if they got together in a room at the station? If, say, Derek Bell had his knife back. It would be an accident of course. Nothing we could have done about it. He'd leave Quentin like a gutted fish. I'm just thinking out loud, of course."

"Obviously if that happened," Jake took up the thought, "Derek Bell would have to die as well."

"Obviously," said Barry.

"It would be a sad thing," Jake put in.

"But unavoidable," concluded Barry. "Our friend Quentin's a danger to society, after all. Very odd. It's only a matter of time before he goes wild, so we'd be saving everybody a lot of trouble."

"Community service," Jake offered.

"It's our duty," concluded Barry, summarising the discussion.

"Derek's knife's in the evidence cupboard, but it could find its way back upstairs," mused Jake.

"Are we sure we want to do this?" Barry asked, opening the canvas bag and peering inside. He held it open for his compatriot to cast his greedy eyes into its black depths and they stood unmoved and staring for several minutes.

An hour later they crept through the rear door of the station. Barry went to the evidence cupboard, found the knife and quietly moved back upstairs. He made sure that nobody else was around and slipped silently into the main interview room. He left the knife on the table with its handle barely but significantly visible, poking from beneath a folder. He stepped innocently back into the corridor. Jake brought Derek Bell up to the door and ushered him inside. Bell's hands were cuffed in front of him.

"I don't see why the hell you're holding me," Bell protested as he obeyed the instruction to sit. His thinning hair was greasy and stuck out in all directions. His clothes were muddy and looked like they hadn't been washed in months.

"Sit down and shut up," Barry ordered. "We're holding you because Quentin Legard saw you with the canvas bags on the moor earlier. He deliberately referred to more than one bag.

"That freak?" roared Bell, beginning to rise from the chair. Barry shoved him back down roughly.

"He recognised you. Even mentioned that tattoo there on your arm, which by the way is the ugliest woman I've ever seen. He said he thought it's your mother." Barry was trying to get under Bell's skin and was succeeding.

Jake said, "we've got to go downstairs for a minute. The duty solicitor's arrived and we need to talk to him. Then he'll want to talk to you, so just wait here and don't cause a fuss."

They stepped outside and locked the door. Barry cocked his head and heard the shuffle as their prisoner moved to the table. He smiled at his partner. At the end of the corridor, thick with August heat and moisture, they found Quentin Legard sitting at another table drinking from a plastic cup.

"Ah," said Barry, "just the man. We've got one or two more questions if you would."

"After you, sir," Jake said, gesturing with his hand.

Quentin Legard took another sip of water and preceded the two policemen down the hall towards the interview room.

Barry whispered to Jake, "he'll scream, but we'll have to give them time."

Jake unlocked the door. "You go on, we'll be in shortly."

Quentin Legard hesitated because he had heard a noise from the room. He put his hand on the door and was about to enter when somebody called his name. Barry and Jake spun round to see two men in suits walking up the hall. They recognised the meaning of men in suits immediately.

"Detective Porter. Hello," Quentin said cheerfully.

Jake realised with a racing heart that Legard knew at least one of the strangers, but couldn't think how. Barry, for his part, couldn't think at all. He was frozen. Shit for brains. The detective was a tall, sombre man with short hair in a monk's fringe just above his narrow eyes. He and the other detectives flourished their badges for the avoidance of doubt.

Jake roused himself and said, "Quentin, let's go back to another room."

Legard either didn't recognise the hint or chose to ignore it and said, "but you wanted me to go into this room. It's probably cooler in there." His hand indicated the room in which Derek Bell and his knife waited.

"No!" Barry shouted, but Quentin Legard pushed past him, entered the room and closed the door behind him.

"What's the matter?" asked Detective Porter.

"Well, nothing," Barry said, far too quickly.

Both Barry and Jake found themselves staring at the door, behind which Legard was probably being stabbed to death at that moment. They forced their attention back to the two suited newcomers, wondering how to salvage the appalling situation. It was quiet in there. Too quiet they knew. Perhaps Bell had slit Legard's throat and was trying to escape through the window.

"Let's go inside," suggested Detective Porter, nodding at the door. "We all need a word about the case and, besides, it's cooler in there, apparently."

Derek Bell was sitting in a chair with his legs stretched out in front of him, resting his cuffed hands in his lap. Sitting across the table was Quentin Legard, flipping through a battered magazine. Ironically, it was an ancient copy of a police procedure manual. The knife was just where Barry had left it. Barry looked at Jake and said a quiet prayer of thanks. Silence filled the room like a lethal creeping gas, and they both waited for the inevitable explosion. Jake was the first to recover his senses.

"I suppose you're wondering why this suspect is here, Detective Porter. I have to admit there's been a mix up. Barry, correct me if I'm wrong, but wasn't the duty solicitor supposed to be here by now?"

Barry recognised his cue. "That's what I thought."

"Mix up? What suspect?" Porter asked.

"Um, well, Derek Bell here."

"You'd better charge me or release me," Bell barked, "and I mean now!"

Porter asked, "who's he? What's he doing here?"

"Well, we arrested him for the robbery tonight," Barry replied.

"You did? Why?" asked the detective.

"Why? Umm," was al Barry could muster.

A third plain clothes officer entered the room and handed a file to Porter, who read its contents carefully, nodded and looked up.

"Ok," said Porter.

Barry shivered with relief and turned a sly smile on Bell. "Thought you'd get off, didn't you?"

Before he had time to add to the thought, Jake and Barry had their arms forcibly restrained and their wrists handcuffed. Even the riot batons were removed. The "Ok" had been a signal meant for the detectives alone. The 'right to remain silent' litany was intoned before the pair had realised what was happening.

"What on earth is going on?" demanded Jake, full of righteous indignation.

"We had a team go through the getaway car. Both your fingerprints were all over it. We also found dozens of footprints that seem to belong to police issue boots leading down to the water near Mr Legard's house. I'll bet they match yours."

"We backed the car out, to search it," protested Barry, whining now.

"Without gloves? Without a crime scene unit present?" Detective Porter pointed out the errors.

"Well, it was obvious; an easy case to solve." Barry whined again.

"There's also the small matter of ninety thousand pounds in the back of your own car." Porter seemed to be enjoying himself now.

"We just didn't have a chance to log it in. What with all the excitement," Barry explained.

"Check out those bags," Jake put in. "They'll have Quentin's fingerprints all over them."

"Actually, they don't," Detective Porter said calmly. "The only prints belong to you two. Oh, and there's a ski mask and a baseball bat, both with DNA matches to fibres found in the armoured car."

"Wait; it's a set up. You haven't got a case here. It's all circumstantial!" Barry's panic was on show for all to see.

"I'm afraid not. We have an eyewitness."

"Who?" Jake asked, glancing towards the corridor.

"Quentin, are these the men you saw walking by the river near your house just after the robbery this afternoon?" asked Detective Porter.

Legard looked from Barry to Jake and back again. "Yes, they are," he affirmed quietly.

"You liar!" Jake cried.

"Were they in uniform, just like now?" Porter continued.

"Yes they were," Legard confirmed.

"What the hell's going on here?" demanded Barry.

Jake choked faintly and turned a cold eye toward Quentin.

"Gentlemen, we're transferring you. You can make your obligatory phone calls from there," Porter announced without emotion.

"He's lying!" Barry shouted. "He told us he couldn't really identify who he saw."

"Well, he's hardly likely to tell you that you're the ones he saw, is he?" Porter reasoned. "With two uniformed bullies with batons standing over him? He was terrified enough telling us the truth."

"No, listen to me!" Jake was pleading now. "You don't understand. He's just out to get us because we picked on him at school."

One of the other detectives sniggered. "Pathetic. Take them away."

Barry and Jake disappeared, their complaints lingering behind them.

Porter removed the handcuffs from Derek Bell. "You're free to go."

The scrawny man glanced around the room and stalked outside.

"May I go too?" Quentin asked.

"Of course, sir. I bet it's been a long day," he said as they shook hands.

-4-

Quentin Legard listened to his music. Usually, late at night, he listened to Debussy or Ravel; something soothing. Tonight, however, was different. Tonight he was playing Holst's Mars from The Planet Suite. It was mean and moody with a resonant and insistent depth that reflected his emotions. He was at war. He listened to classical music all day long, through expensive Bang and Olufsen high end speakers. He often laughed to himself, recalling the time he overheard somebody in town mention the 'satanic music' he listened to. He wasn't sure what the particular piece could have been, but the timing of the comment suggested it may have been Rachmaninoff.

He walked through the house, shutting off the lights, though he left on the picture lights illuminating a favourite Jackson Pollock. He had to get to Paris soon. A dealer friend had acquired two small Picassos and had promised Quentin first choice. He also missed Jeanette; he hadn't seen her in a month and familiar feelings were beginning to stir within him. It was nearly midnight as he sat down in his mother's rocking chair and gazed upward where the black of the trees became the black of the heavens, and a brilliant dusting of stars spread out in a hemisphere above him. He sat this way for some minutes, taking pleasure in the constellations and the moon.

He heard the footsteps long before he saw the figure moving up the path.

"Hey," he called.

"Hey," Derek Bell called back.

He climbed the stairs, panting, and dropped four heavy canvas bags at his feet. He sat, as he always did, not in one of the chairs but on the floor, supporting himself against the wall.

"You left over ninety thousand?" Quentin asked.

"Sorry," Derek said, cringing, ever deferential to his boss. "I counted wrong."

Quentin laughed. "That was probably a good idea."

He had thought Barry and Jake would possibly have fallen for the scam if they put as little as thirty or forty thousand by the waterfall and in the getaway car, but wave double a man's salary, tax free, in front of his face and nine times out of ten you've definitely bought him. However, with a job this big it was a good idea to have a little extra bait. Quentin and Derek would still clear almost £400,000.

"We'll have to sit on it for a while, even though it's cash," Derek said.

"Yes, we'll need to be really careful with this one," Quentin confirmed.

Usually, they only operated in places far away from their homes, but when Quentin had learned from an inside man that such a large cash transfer was to be made he could not resist the temptation. He knew the guards would be lightweights and had probably never handled anything so important. The money was appealing, of course. What tipped the scales, however, was that Quentin thought that in order to make the scam work he needed two unwitting participants, preferably policemen. He didn't have any doubt whom to pick; adolescent grudges last as long as those of spurned lovers.

"Did you have to hurt him?" Quentin asked, meaning the guard. One of his rules was that there should be no violence unless absolutely necessary.

"He was no trouble," replied Derek. "I only broke a rib or two."

"Quentin nodded. He gazed at the sky, hoping to see a shooting star.

"Do you feel sorry for them?" Derek asked, after a moment.

"Who, the guards?" replied Quentin.

"No, Barry and Jake," replied Derek Bell.

Quentin considered this for a while. The music, the fragrant late summer air and the rhythmic symphony of insect had turned him philosophical.

"I'm thinking about something Barry said. About how I didn't see eye to eye with him and Jake. He was talking about the robbery, but what he was really talking about was my life and theirs, whether he knew it or not. I don't think he did, but it makes sense," he reflected. "It sums up quite well the difference between us. Our musical tastes are different, I'll bet, for example. I could have lived with it if they had just gone their own way, in school and afterwards. But they didn't. No. They made an issue of it at every opportunity. Too bad. It was their choice, and we all have to live with our own choices."

"Well, I'm glad you didn't see eye to eye," said Derek. "Here's to differences."

"To differences," responded Quentin Legard as the two men clinked their wine glasses together and drank appreciatively.

"Do you know why we clink glasses?" asked Derek.

"As a matter of fact I do," said Quentin.

"Really?" Bell kept it short, as he realised the mistake he had made. He prayed that his friend would not launch into one of his legendary history lessons.

His prayers were not answered as the learned, erudite Quentin Legard began his diatribe.

"Humans throughout history have made a habit of basing a great deal of our traditions and customs around food. The curious practice of raising our drink containers is one of the most ancient of these. Let's begin by dispelling a myth."

"Yes, let's," Derek whispered without any enthusiasm at all, as he took a sip.

Quentin ignored his friend's lack of enthusiasm.

"You may have heard that the tradition of toasting originated out of a fear of poisoning; the idea being that clinking two glasses together would cause the liquid from both to spill into one another; thus, the people you're drinking with wouldn't poison you as they'd then be poisoning themselves. As interesting as this historical rumour is, not surprisingly, there is not a single shred of evidence backing up this conjecture.

As to the real origin, because the practice of honouring through a drink offering seems to have begun in pre-history, it's hard to say who first got the idea. In fact, most ancient societies show evidence of doing this. The Ancient Greeks would offer libations to the Gods as a ritualistic practice, as well as make a point of drinking to each other's health. Evidence of this can be found in *The Odyssey* when Ulysses drinks to the health of Achilles. The Romans placed such an importance on drinking to health that at one point in time the Senate passed a decree that stated that all must drink to Emperor Augustus at every meal. 'The Decline and Fall of The Roman Empire even describes a feast where Attila the Hun indulges in at least three toasts for every course."

Derek groaned as Quentin warmed to his task.

"The term *"toast"* itself originated in the 16th century. One of the first written accounts of it was in Shakespeare's The Merry Wives of Windsor when the character of Falstaff demands – *"Go fetch me a quart of sack; put a toast in't."* To translate, he's asking for a great deal of wine with, literally, a piece of toast in it. I can hear your disgusted outrage and objections to adding toast to wine, but it was actually quite a common practice at the time. This is thought to be due to the quality of wine in the past; it was in many cases inferior to our modern vintages. Thus, placing a piece of toast within a jug was supposed to soak up some of the acidity and improve the flavour. This also had the side benefit of giving people something to do with a piece of stale bread, often spiced or with fruit embedded in it, which would improve the bread's palatability. Up until very recently in history, wasting food just wasn't something people tended to do, so finding ways to make stale bread taste good was fairly common- waste not, want not. (This was also more or less how French Toast got its start.)"

Derek Bell was quickly losing the will to live and said, "please, that's enough. You're giving me headache. I can't take in all these facts at one go."

"But I've barely begun, said his friend. "There's loads more."

"Let's leave something for another time," pleaded Derek.

"If you're sure," said Quentin.

"Oh, I'm sure," asserted Derek.

"Ok," said Quentin "we'll leave the history lesson for another day. Now let's see let's see what the future holds," he whispered as he leaned forward to divide the cash into two equal piles.

THE EARLY DAYS
-5-

The headlights lit the sensuous sweep of the road ahead of her as she cruised through the woodlands, swaying left and right. The evening was damp and it had been a cold spring. Her Mercedes drifted over the white line marking the middle of the road and the Lane Keeping Assist, part of the optional Driver Assistance Package, warned her with pulsed vibrations on the steering wheel. Her reverie disturbed, she asked herself whether she'd had two glasses of wine or three. She decided it had only been two and pressed the accelerator. She used this road every morning and evening and she always thought of it as having sensuous curves.

Her mood was sombre tonight as she drove in her bare feet. She convinced herself it gave her a better feel for the car, but the real reason was that she refused to allow her expensive high heels to get scuffed. She looked across at them on the passenger seat and smiled at her white spike heeled shoes, resting there. She liked expensive things; they made her feel good. They made her feel that she was achieving something with her life. Above all, it boosted her self-esteem.

Twelve miles from home Charlotte gently lifted her foot off the accelerator, coaxed the car through the final set of, yes, sensuous curves, and entered the last stretch of straight road that would take her up a slight incline past the village green and into the village itself. The small development was hundreds of years old and had been much more significant in its heyday. Now, however, there remained only a petrol station, which was struggling bravely to survive the harsh economic climate, a small shop and post office, the obligatory pub and a church. In fact that is true in hundreds of villages across the country, and in her mind she imagined the congregation straining at the leash to finish a service so that their drinking time was not restricted. It further amused her that the pub had four rooms. Either tourism was on the increase or some locals wanted to sleep off their drinking habits away from the prying eyes of family or friends. There was also an antique shop. Charlotte always wondered how it kept going as she had never seen anybody buy a single item in the five years that she had been passing that way.

She slowed to thirty as she approached the village green and its gravelled car park, for this was where she knew the local traffic police lurked, ambush predators hidden from view, ready to pounce upon unsuspecting motorists in order to ensure their monthly speeding targets were met.

She had developed the habit of stopping at the petrol station each evening on her way home. Sometimes she needed petrol, but she always bought coffee to take away. It was a strangely modern service for such an antiquated place. She reached across for her heels and slipped them on. As she climbed out of the car she saw another customer, a man with a five o'clock shadow leaning against his car, talking on his mobile phone. He nodded unhappily. Whoever was speaking on the other end was delivering bad news. Charlotte rattled the nozzle into her filler and clicked the catch on the handle so that it automatically controlled the flow and would cut off when necessary. She stood up and felt a chill. She was wearing an expensive jacket which was cut low, no blouse and a short skirt. With some satisfaction she noticed the customer's eyes lift from the tarmac and scan her body.

She realised the facial shadow was in fact designer stubble and he was also dressed well in a smooth grey suit and dark trench coat with a multitude of flaps. His car was a Lexus, gun metal in colour and she calculated that it probably cost as much as her Mercedes. She approved of men in expensive cars. The snap of the nozzle shutting itself off disturbed her. She made sure that she was noticed as she swayed inside to pay for the fuel and a coffee. Without a hint of recognition the young assistant looked up from his portable TV just long enough to cast an appraising glance at her chest while he gave her the change. She wondered whether he always recognised people solely from that part of their anatomy, or was she the only one. It was a flattering thought.

She stepped back outside, glancing at the man with the Lexus as he tossed his phone onto the seat of his car and thrust his hand deep into his pocket, fishing for cash. He looked at her again. Then he froze, his eyes widening, focussing just past her. In the next instant she felt an arm snake around her waist and cold metal at her ear.

"Oh, God!"

"Sh, sh, shut up!" a young man's voice stuttered in her ear. He was nervous and smelled of whisky. "Get in the car. You scream and I'll kill you."

Charlotte had never been mugged. She'd lived in London and briefly in Manchester, but the only time she had felt physically threatened was one evening when the couple in the apartment across the hall had argued violently and the man had stormed out brandishing a heavy metal frying pan. She was now paralyzed with fear as the mugger dragged her toward her car.

"Please, just take the keys," she screamed.

"No way. I want you as much as the car."

"Please, no!" she moaned. "I'll give you money."

"Shut up. You're coming with me," her attacker whispered into her ear.

"No, she's not."

The man with the Lexus had walked unnoticed to the passenger side of the Mercedes and was standing between them and her car. His eyes were steady and he didn't seem at all afraid. Her attacker, on the other hand, appeared terrified.

"Get out of the way!" he shouted as he shoved his knife forward. "Move! Nobody'll get hurt if you do what I say."

"If you want a car, take it. In fact why not take mine? It's almost new. There's only a few thousand miles on the clock." The Lexus man held up his keys.

"I'm taking her and her car and you're getting out of my way," the mugger shouted again. "I don't want to use this knife, but I will."

The sharp point wavered in the hand of the thin, almost emaciated, young man with his dishwater brown hair, tied back in a ponytail.

The man from the Lexus smiled and continued to talk calmly. "Look, my friend, taking a car is one thing, kidnapping or rape is completely different. Forget about it. You'll go away forever."

"Get the hell out my way! His voice cracked now.

He moved forward a few feet, forcing Charlotte along with him. She was whimpering; hating herself for it but she had lost all control. The Lexus man stood his ground and the youth shoved the knife directly at his face. What happened next happened quickly, but she saw it in agonisingly slow motion. The man from the Lexus turned his palms towards the mugger in a gesture of surrender, stepping back slightly. The passenger door swung open and the mugger shoved her inside roughly. She realised crazily that she had never even sat on the passenger seat before. She felt it was too far forward and feared tearing her skirt and scuffing her shoes. Her attacker walked around the front of the car to the driver's side, forcing his opponent, his hands still raised, out of the way. Charlotte looked hopelessly into the petrol station window, but the young attendant was still behind the counter, still eating crisps, still watching his tiny TV.

The mugger started to climb into the car. He paused, looked back and realised the fuel nozzle was still in the petrol filler. At that precise moment the Lexus man lunged, grabbing the mugger's knife hand. He gasped in surprise and fought fiercely to free his hand, but the other man was stronger. Charlotte wrestled her door open and sprang out as the two men tumbled onto the front of the Mercedes, grappling for the knife. The bony attacker felt his wrist being hammered onto the car's windscreen until it eventually flew from his grip. Charlotte squinted as it landed at her high heeled feet. She never held a knife like that in her life. Indeed, she hardly ever even used a knife in the kitchen, so privileged had her life been.

She crouched down, lifted it and felt its heavy, balanced weight. She felt its awful capacity to harm. She shoved the point towards the stomach of the mugger and he went limp as cloth. Her saviour was a good foot taller than the attacker. He rolled off the bonnet of the Mercedes and took the ponytailed youth by the collar. Charlotte held her threatening posture, but her eyes betrayed her. Her hand began to tremble.

"Just push it in," her saviour said, encouraging her.

She was paralysed with fear and uncertainty and both men knew she would not use the knife. Her attacker realised it first and, pushing the Lexus man away with surprising strength, took off at a gallop into the bushes beside the petrol station. He was gone in an instant. In the distance a car started; a car with a distinctive rattle to its exhaust. A screech of complaining tyres ripped the air.

-6-

"Oh God, Oh God," was all Charlotte could manage as she closed her eyes and leaned against her car.

"Are you alright?" he asked.

She nodded. "Yes. No. I don't know. What can I say? Thank you." Tears welled and her entire body shook. Unwittingly she still held the knife at waist height, pointing forwards. "Oh, sorry."

She offered it to him, but he glanced down and said, "you'd better hold onto it until the police get here. I'm not supposed to have much to do with such things."

Charlotte didn't understand. For a moment she thought he was in recovery and touching a weapon would be like an alcoholic taking a drink. She wondered whether people got addicted to weapons in the same way that other people, her husband for example, became addicted to gambling, drugs or sex. Her confusion must have shown.

"I have a record," he said simply. He said it without shame or pride in a tone that suggested he was used to mentioning it early in a conversation, getting the fact out of the way, and assessing the reaction. Charlotte had no reaction and he continued, "if somebody finds me with a knife it would be a problem."

"Oh," she said, as if he were a checkout worker explaining why an expired voucher couldn't be used.

His eyes dipped again to her jacket. Well, more accurately to the part of her body where her jacket was absent. He glanced inside the petrol station where the assistant continued watching his TV in unconcerned oblivion.

"We'd better call the police; he's not going to," he said.

"Wait," she said. "Can I ask you a question?"

"Of course," he replied.

"What did you do time for?"

"Well," he said slowly, deciding whether Charlotte, with her beautiful jacket, short skirt, designer heels and fragrant perfume could ever be his. He concluded that to be unlikely, so he had nothing to lose. "Assault with a deadly weapon, five charges and I was guilty of them all. Oh, and conspiracy to commit assault. So, should we call the police?"

"No," she answered firmly, slipping the knife into the glove compartment of her car. "I think we should have a drink," she said and nodded towards the front door of the pub across the road.

They awoke three hours later. He looked like a smoker but he wasn't. He looked like a drinker too and drink they had, but he'd had only one beer to her three gins and tonic. They stared at the cracked ceiling.

"Do you have somewhere you have to be?" she asked.

"Doesn't everybody?" he replied, enigmatically.

"I mean now. Tonight," she continued.

"No," he replied. "I'm just in the area for the day. I'm going back home tomorrow. Home, he'd explained over the earlier drinks, was Exmoor. His name was Lawrence; emphatically not Larry. After prison he'd gone straight and given up his job of collecting debts for some people he described vaguely as 'local businessmen.' Then she asked for his surname. His eyes went cloudy and after some thought he said, "Anderson." He might just as well have answered "Smith." He said, "none of the above," to her inquiry about a wife and family and she was inclined to believe him. He was simply, well, overwhelming. That was the only way she could describe it. His strong arms around her; his body atop hers. As they lay now in the warm, cheap bed, she watched his chest rise and fall. There was a nasty scar on it, clearly visible beneath the hair. She wanted to ask him about it but couldn't summon the courage.

"Lawrence?"

He glanced at her cautiously. This was that revered moment after making love. A risky time. Certain conventions had to be observed; routines followed. Honesty could be dangerous, but sincerity was a must. Synonyms for 'commitment' and 'love and 'the future,' if not in those exact words, had ruined many an evening.

Charlotte's mind was not on any of those matters. She was picturing the sharp knife in her glove compartment and the high, frantic voice of the man who'd almost kidnapped her.

"What do you do for a living now?" she asked him.

"I'm between jobs at the moment," he answered after a long pause. "I'm really what you could call a 'Contract Consultant.' I used to do various things. He paused, debating whether to embellish his history or leave it at that. He decided that was enough. She remembered his sullen face during the conversation on his mobile phone and didn't pursue the subject.

"Can I ask you a question?" he asked.

"Certainly," she replied. "I'm married, no children, I love sex and I drink too much. Anything else?"

He grinned. "That about covers it, I think. Oh, why didn't you want to call the police?"

Instead of answering she asked, "why were you so calm back there?"

He shrugged. "I've had plenty of knives pulled on me and I can tell when somebody's going to actually use one and when he's not. If he'd been a pro I'd have said goodbye and good luck and hoped the police got to you before it was too late."

"Have you ever killed anybody?"

His silence was his answer. "No more questions from you till you answer mine," he said after a long pause. "Why no police?"

"Because I have a business proposition for you," she replied without hesitation.

"You want a contract drawn up? Are you selling or buying? He asked.

"I'm buying. It's a sort of contract," she said as she turned to look into his eyes. "I want you to murder my husband."

"Divorce him," he said. "It's much easier and it's what lawyers are for. If he's worth a lot of money and he's cheating, you'll get at least half."

"Well," Charlotte began reluctantly.

"Ah. He's not the only guilty party," said Lawrence, laughing and gesturing toward the bed they were now sharing. "Who cheated first?"

"He did!" she rushed the answer. "Well, he got caught first anyway," she added.

"Marriage can be much like having a prostate examination, you know," he said. "It's something which leaves you wanting to be on your own for a while," he added.

He allowed the homespun philosophy time to be digested and understood before saying, "I think you've misread me. I'm not a hitman; never have been."

"What can I say to convince you?" she asked.

"Nothing. Not a thing," he replied.

"So, what can I do to convince you?" She moved her hands along his body, stopped to pinch his thigh playfully, and continued on her travels. He laughed but he stopped smiling when she said, "fifty thousand."

He pretended to be thoughtful for a moment. "No, I've done my time and I didn't like it one bit.

The hesitation was probably only a fraction of a second, but to Charlotte it was plenty long enough. "A hundred."

Lawrence said, "I don't think so."

"I don't think so," she repeated his words. "That's not the same as no."

"It's not easy killing somebody. Well, that's not quite true. The killing is the easy part; it's getting away with it that's difficult. Almost impossible most of the time, I'd say."

"Well now," she persevered, "I'm hearing 'almost' and 'most of the time.' All that tells me that it's do-able."

"Have you ever threatened to kill him?" he asked.

She shrugged. "I found him with his girlfriend once. I just lost it and shouted and screamed that I'd kill them both.

Actually, that's not true. I think I said they'd wish they were dead by the time I finished with them."

"Ouch," he responded.

"I don't think anybody heard me," she ventured.

"Well," he said slowly, like a doctor formulating an opinion, "you've got a reason to kill him, but that's a problem in itself. It means you've got to find a fall guy. You've got to make it look like it's more likely that somebody else committed the crime than you, even if you have a motive. We need to find another suspect."

"Mmm," she smiled and eased her breasts against him. "Such as a mugger or car thief?"

"Yes," he smiled in return, his eyes returning towards the petrol station. "We've got his knife and it's got his fingerprints all over it, but we'd have to wipe it."

"Why?" she asked, mystified.

"You picked it up, remember."

"Oh, I forgot," she replied, feeling rather stupid.

"Do you really want to have him charged with murder? It seems a bit extreme; after all, he was only trying to steal your car," he said.

"Oh yes!" Charlotte affirmed. "He was going to rape me, remember."

"Oh, I forgot," he said, mocking her earlier lapse of memory.

"We could always look at it as doing a good deed, putting him away before he really hurts someone. Or doing him a favour and saving him."

He gazed up at the ceiling. To Charlotte it seemed he was lost in thought, running through an embryonic plan; ironing out the wrinkles.

"We'd have to set it up carefully. Do you know where he goes with his girlfriend?" he asked.

"I've already told you; I found them together once. I'm sure they always go to the same place."

"How does it work?" he laughed. "I was married for ten years and never had an affair. Would she leave the place first? Or him?"

"She'd leave first. He'd have to wait and pay for the room," Charlotte said.

"Ok. After he pays for the room, I could be waiting for him," he continued to pull her in.

"And you kill him!" she exclaimed with an unnatural degree of enthusiasm.

"In a motel car park, with people around. Are you trying to send me to jail? No, I'll force him to drive to a deserted place and do it there. I'll make it look as though we fought and I killed him. Then I panicked and jumped out of the car. I'll drop the knife on the way and you follow and pick me up."

"When do you want to do it?" Charlotte had already made up her mind.

"As soon as possible," replied Lawrence. "I could do with a hundred thousand at the moment."

He didn't divulge the reasons for his current need for money, but his enthusiasm was enough for Charlotte.

"Steve usually goes to see her on Tuesday and Thursday nights," she said. "Today's Tuesday. I bet that's where he is now."

"No, it's too quick. I need time to plan a bit. Let's go for the day after tomorrow. It looks like a good plan. We've got a murder weapon that can't be traced to us, a good motive and a fall guy," he said, looking deeply into her eyes as if trying to reach her soul and test it.

Lawrence had taken control and it thrilled her. Charlotte rolled on top of him once more. She straddled him, feeling his interest in her toned body rapidly reviving. As they grew increasingly passionate she was thinking that she had found her fall guy and his motive was his need for money.

"I think it'll work," he said.

"So do I," she agreed and began to chew on his lower lip as, united, they rocked gently back and forth.

-7-

Thursday arrived and brought with it another overcast evening. Charlotte was wearing a long sleeved navy blouse and a pleated skirt that ended halfway between knee and ankle. A couple of work colleagues had looked with surprise as there was no cleavage and no thigh on display. Neither were there any straining buttons and her hair was pulled back in a plain ponytail. She'd decided that after she had made the anonymous call to the police reporting the disturbance at the motel, she'd have to rush home and prepare to be the demure, innocent widow as she may not have time to change her clothes. She found herself in an odd state. She was nearly aroused. The swaying of the car, the sensuous bends, the cool air on her skin and, she had to admit, the thought of Steve dying, turned her on. So did getting her hands on his money. He was such a miser. He wouldn't even buy her the Mercedes; it had to be leased. She thought about Lawrence too. He was such a great lover, but he'd be an even better fall guy. It wouldn't be easy, though. She couldn't call the police from the car, of course, as there would be a record.

She decided to pick the place for herself. It would make sense to Lawrence because she knew the area better than him. She planned to follow him after he had killed Steve and was on his way to meet her. When he left his car to phone her she would slip out of her own car and flatten the rear tyre on Steve's car with the kitchen knife she had in her bag. The she'd leave Lawrence there and rush to the local shop, raise the alarm and call the police. Lawrence would be trapped. It would be take him half an hour to get out on foot, but the police would be there in a matter of minutes. It was perfect. Her thoughts moved to the hotel, where her husband was right at the moment and she pictured them in bed together. More specifically, she pictured his girlfriend. Her name was Olivia Sorensen and she was blonde and boringly pretty. When Charlotte had stalked them Olivia was wearing a ludicrous black floppy hat and was walking close to Steve with his elbow hard against her chest. They stopped in front of her as she screamed like a wailing banshee. She really had enjoyed that little scene. She wondered what they were doing at that precise moment, her hands gripping ever more tightly onto the steering wheel. Were they drinking wine? Was he kissing her? Where? Her mind raced along and was flooded by increasingly detailed images.

She almost missed Lawrence's motel. She slowed to a halt a little way past it, as they had agreed, and he stepped out from behind a row of bushes. He climbed into the car before it had actually stopped moving.

"Go!" he snapped as the drama of the event took hold.

She sped back onto the road. She had expected that he'd be dressed in, well, killer clothes. Like a commando, maybe, or at least a black sweater and jeans or something. Instead he was just wearing a business suit under the elaborate trench coat. She saw that he was actually wearing a tie and it was neatly pulled up tight to his collar.

"Are you sure he's at the hotel?" he asked.

"He called and said he was going to be late for dinner. Said he had a meeting with his boss," Charlotte replied.

"How do you know it's a lie?" he asked.

"Because his boss is in London all week. I checked," Charlotte answered, smiling.

Lawrence laughed at the stupidity. "If you're going to lie, you have to make it good. What do you know about his girlfriend?"

Another flashing stab of jealousy coursed through her and she replied, "she's got small boobs and needs a nose job."

"Is she married as well?" Lawrence asked.

"Yes. She's just a rich bitch who inherited daddy's money and thinks she can do whatever she likes. They deserve each other." Charlotte was backing out now.

"Well, let's hope she leaves the room first. It'll be no good having a witness," he said as he pulled on tight fitting cotton work gloves.

"Don't you wear rubber gloves?" she asked.

"No," he replied, "cloth is better. No fingerprints inside.

She realised that Lawrence Anderson, Smith, or whoever, was a thorough man. She opened the glove box and took out the knife.

"Did you wipe it?" he asked.

"No," she said. "I don't know how."

He laughed. "You just.....wipe it." He pulled a damp tissue wipe from its box on her dashboard and carefully wiped the blade and handle.

"There," she said. "There it is." She pointed to the hotel ahead of them, with its red 'vacancies' light pulsing appealingly. It was a seedy place. Charlotte was struck by its contrast to the places where she insisted her lovers took her. They had to be at least bed and breakfast standard. She parked on the street, with a view of the car park and instantly recognised Steve's car. She wondered which car belonged to Olivia.

"Oh," she said, "I've found a good place to do it. It's about five miles from here and deserted." She made it sound as though she had only just thought about it, and Lawrence hoped that was not true. She went on to describe in great detail the location and the route to it.

"Good," Lawrence replied, but he was obviously not listening.

Charlotte was irritated by his apparent lack of attention to her detailed instructions but he ignored her annoyance and issued instructions of his own.

"You stay right here. I'm going to hide in the bushes. I'll get him into the car and drive him there. I'll find a place by the side of the road. You follow us." He was all business now. His intention was to boost her confidence and it worked.

Charlotte took a deep breath. "Ok."

"Afterwards, you drop me at my hotel and go home. When he doesn't show up tonight, call the police. Remember, don't overact when you find out what happened. It's better to look stunned than hysterical. Sort of zoned out."

"Stunned, not hysterical," Charlotte affirmed.

He leaned forward and gripped her neck hard; pulled her lips to his. She kissed back, just as hard. She enjoyed a little shiver, feeling the gloves on her neck. She mused inwardly that it might be fun to dress up sometimes for one of her lovers and looked into his eyes. He released his grip and returned her gaze.

"Good luck," she offered as he climbed out and crouched beside the car.

The area was deserted, but he was still hunched over as he ran through a wedge shaped shadow beside the hotel and disappeared behind a row of trees. Charlotte laid her head against the leather headrest and clicked on the radio. Now, finally, the nervousness descended like a spray of cold rain. The horror of the evening unfurled within her and her hands began to quiver. "What am I doing?" she wondered. The answer came to her: "what I should have done a long time ago." Suddenly her unease turned to rage. "I hate these damn clothes. I want to be dressed up. I want to be going out for nice wine and martinis. I want that idiot Steve out of my life. I want to get the whole thing over."

As her mind raced there was a loud scream from the hotel. Startled, she sat forward staring into the car park at Steve's car. Two more shouts and another scream followed and lights went on in some of the windows. Charlotte felt the fear inside her like a cold stone. She scanned the car park. More lights were being switched on and doors opened. Several people stepped out, looking around. There was motion to her right. She looked towards Lawrence, who was standing in the shadows. His eyes were wide and on his face there was a look of terror. Was he holding his stomach? Had he been hurt? She could not tell.

"What?" Charlotte screamed.

He looked around in panic and gestured frantically to leave. He mouthed, "go...go...get home now." He disappeared back into the bushes. Had a guard or off-duty policeman seen him with the knife? Two people stepped from the manager's office; a fat woman in a blue suit and a skinny man wearing a short-sleeved white shirt. They looked around the building, said something to each other and then listened to other people who were emerging. Charlotte couldn't tell what was being said. She looked back towards where she had last seen Lawrence as he had whispered his warning, but there was no sign of him. She felt the danger on her skin and her brain registered. She decided it was time to leave and slammed her foot on the accelerator. As the car sped forward she heard a soft pop and the unmistakable 'whup, whup, whup' of a tyre going flat. Despite her growing sense of fear and panic she kept going. The hotel guests and the couple from the manager's office were staring at her car as it swerved away. Then the rubber separated from the rim of the wheel and the car jolted to a halt, scraping against the kerb with a tooth aching grind.

"Damn! Damn! Damn!" she screamed, slamming her fist on the steering wheel. In the rear view mirror she saw the flashing lights of a police car as it sped towards the hotel. The young officers glanced at her car but passed it by before parking further up the street. They trotted to the crowd of guests by the manager's office. Several of them pointed to a room on the first floor and the officers hurried away. Other marked cars arrived, followed by the unmistakable shape of an ambulance. She was at a loss. She couldn't choose between running away or staying put. She suddenly realised that her car could be traced and it would be suspicious if she fled. She began to compose a story. 'My husband called me and asked me to meet him here. I happened to see his car.'

The police officers knocked on the door to room 103 and, when there was no answer, the skinny man in the white shirt unlocked it. He stood back as they walked inside slowly. If it was Steve's room, and if Steve was inside, Charlotte guessed he was dead. But what had happened? She was startled as she became aware of a rapping on her window, and she screamed, turning to see a large uniformed shape standing beside her. She stared at him; her mouth open.

"Miss, could you move your car?" he asked politely.

"Oh, you gave me a start. Sorry, the tyre's flat." She spoke in rapid bursts.

"Is there something wrong, madam?" asked the policeman.

"No. Nothing's wrong. I just….it's just that I had a flat tyre," she replied, trying to calm herself.

"Could I see you licence, please?" he asked.

"Why?" she said.

"Your licence, please?" he repeated.

She stared at his uniform and his radio, but didn't move. A moment passed.

"Now," he said, with a degree of sternness. "You are acting strangely. Step out of the car." He ordered.

"Well now, officer," she smiled and leaned towards him, raising her arms together. Only after a glance at his perplexed face did she remember that the attention getting valley between her breasts was hidden by her conservative blue blouse. She climbed out of the car and handed him her licence.

"Have you had a drink today?" he asked.

"No. Well, I had one wine a couple of hours ago. Well, two." She was struggling for composure and the officer saw it.

"I see," he said, as she looked at the offending tyre. "Is this your current address?" he asked.

"Yes," she replied,

Her eyes were on the hotel as more police arrived. There were a dozen cars now, their flashing blue lights rebounding from every surface, catching the scene in strobe effect. Two men in suits stood out. One had bushy hair and the other was balding. The blue flashes reflected from his bald pate in a mixture of the comic and the sinister. Their authority was evident. Charlotte's policeman walked slowly to the back of her car to check the registration number. He seemed calm and reasonable and she was beginning to relax a little. He'd let her go, she thought. She was sure. It'll be alright. Just stay calm and they'll never put anything together. Then his radio crackled and he listened intently to the message. She felt the change as his eyes turned to her. He didn't blink and turned her licence over in one hand.

"Oh, Jesus," Charlotte whispered to herself as the officer called to one of the two detectives.

In no time at all she was sitting in the back of a patrol car, albeit without handcuffs. She had been told to stay there. A young uniformed officer came running up to the detective and handed him a large plastic bag containing the knife that Lawrence had apparently dropped as he fled.

"What have we got here?" he said.

Charlotte prayed that Lawrence had remembered to wipe the knife.

"What's this?" asked the detective, pointing to something white caught on the handle of the knife. "There's something here. It looks like a bit of tissue." He examined it closely. "Yes. It's a bit of tissue."

Charlotte looked on in horror as she saw the detective walked to her Mercedes, retrieve something and come back.

"Look what I've found." He pointed to the wad of white tissue that Lawrence had dropped on the floor after he'd wiped the knife. Her mind raced. Well. So what? There were hundreds of thousands of boxes of tissues around the country. How could they prove anything? Her eyes widened as the detective carefully separated the wad of tissue to reveal a triangular tear in the middle. He knew the scrap caught on the handle of the knife would fit like the final piece of a jigsaw puzzle. Another officer came up to the detectives holding the cloth gloves Lawrence had worn. The bushy haired detective lifted them and smelled the palm. Charlotte could smell the scent too and she started to hyperventilate. She knew all the policemen were staring at her as handcuffs were produced and she was asked to stand and turn around. She felt the cold hardness as they were locked in place around her slender wrists.

"No, no. you don't understand," she cried as her rights were intoned and she was pushed back into a car. She heard a faint squealing of tyres in the distance. She stared at the approaching car but her mind was elsewhere. 'Let's work it out,' she thought. 'Let's say Lawrence and the mugger are in this together. Maybe the mugger is a friend of his. They steal Steve's knife. I stop for coffee and petrol. They could have followed me and found out I stop there every night. They make it look like a mugging. I sleep with Lawrence. But why? What's he up to? Who is he?'

At that moment the car that had been speeding towards the hotel skidded to a stop nearby. Lawrence leapt out, leaving the door open, and ran in panic towards the doorway of room 103.

"No! No! My wife." He shouted.

A uniformed officer restrained him and pulled him back from the door. He was sobbing.

"I came as soon as you called. I can't believe it. No! No! No!"

The officer's arm slipped around the shoulders of the fancy navy blue trench coat and he led the sobbing man back to the detectives, who gazed at him with sympathy.

The bald one asked, "is your name Sorensen?"

"That's right," he said, struggling to control his grief. "Lawrence Sorensen." Breathlessly he asked, "you mean....she was cheating on me? And somebody killed her?"

Unseen by any officer he cast a glance at Charlotte. It was a look that could only be described as amused as the dawning realisation crept its way across her face. She remembered then something he had told her.

"You've got to make it look like it's more likely that somebody else committed the crime than you, even if you have a motive, Charlotte."

She was never to know that she had become one of the many victims, not of a man named Lawrence Anderson, Smith or Sorensen. His real name was Quentin Legard and his legend was taking shape.

LEGARD THE ENFORCER
-8-

The husband and wife made their way quickly through the dark streets in the suburbs south of the river. The local authority had decided in its wisdom to have the street lights turned off after midnight as part of its cost cutting measures and the result was stygian darkness. They concentrated carefully on where they put their feet as they had both had unfortunate experiences thanks to the generosity of lazy dog owners.

The summer air was cool and Carolyn wore a coat to make up for her light attire underneath. She was wearing a low cut blouse, with an expensive gold necklace adorning her neck, and a skirt which ended at around knee level. Her heels, whilst not overly high, meant that she felt better with her hand being held by her husband's strong and protective grip. Charlie was wearing a smart green shirt, dark trousers and he too chose to use a coat as protection from the chill.

"I enjoyed that," she said, holding tightly to his arm as they negotiated a crook in the narrow road.

"Thank you."

The couple greatly enjoyed their visits to the local theatre, whether it was to see plays or concerts. Charlie's wine-importing company had struggled long and hard during the recession and had only recently begun to show a profit, so the Morgans had had little money to spend on their own amusements. Indeed, until this year, they had been forced to content themselves with not going out at all. It had therefore been a surprise to Carolyn when her husband had come home one day and told her that he had booked for them to see her favourite singer and he had arranged the best seats in the house. His industry was at last showing some rewards as the country as a whole began to emerge from austerity and its people started to smile again.

A shout from behind startled them and Charlie turned to see, perhaps fifteen yards away, a man dressed in black from head to toe. The man had been so intent on crossing the road that he hadn't noticed the oncoming vehicle, which swerved violently to avoid him. Perhaps it was Charlie's imagination, or a trick of the light, but it appeared to him that the pedestrian looked up, noted Charlie's gaze and turned with haste into an alleyway. Not wishing to alarm his wife, though, he made no mention of the man and continued his conversation.

"How about going to the West End to see a show next month?"

Carolyn laughed. "I'd like that, but are you sure we can afford it?"

"I think we could run to that," Charlie said with a smile for his wife.

He glanced behind them once more but saw no sign of the man in black. As they turned the corner onto the road that would take them to the bridge across the river, however, the very man appeared from an adjacent alleyway. He had flanked their route at a run, it seemed, and now stepped forward, breathing hard.

"I'm sorry to intrude and I apologise if I have frightened you, but I'd like to speak to you."

Charlie assumed the man was a beggar and was wary. The city could be a dangerous place and beggars often turned nasty if they didn't get what they wanted. Charlie put his hand into his coat pocket and withdrew a knife, making sure he stood between the man and Carolyn. His wife let out a high pitched shriek and stepped further away from the two men.

"Please, there's no need for that," the man in black said quickly, "I don't want to harm you and I'm not armed. That is to say, I'm only armed with the truth."

He was a strange looking man. His eyes were sunken into his skull and his skin had a jaundiced yellow hue. He appeared to all intents and purposes incapable of the physical effort to cause another man any harm. Indeed, to Charlie, he seemed near to drawing his final breath. His coat looked to have been stolen from somebody considerably fatter than him as it hung loosely from his bony, emaciated skeletal figure.

"Who are you?" Charlie demanded, holding his knife at the ready. He was not a violent man, but would do whatever was necessary to protect himself and his wife.

"I'm a stage hand at the theatre you've been to this evening. That's why I'm dressed in black." The stranger whispered huskily, before hawking and spitting on the pavement.

Charlie noticed that the man smelled somewhat and backed away a little. "What do you want? I'll phone the police if you don't get out of the way," he added, and used his other hand to fish his mobile phone from his coat pocket.

"Please, there's no need for that," the man in black repeated. "There's really no need, Mr Morgan."

"You know me!" Charlie was startled.

"Yes I do; very well actually," the stagehand said as his yellow eyes grew troubled. "I'll be honest. My name is Parr and I have until recently lived an evil life."

Carolyn shivered as the chill night air began to penetrate her coat.

"I would have continued with my awful life but for the Lord our God appearing to me in a dream two weeks ago."

Charlie's face reflected his scepticism. He had never believed in things like that.

"No, please let me explain," said the man in black. "He told me to make amends for my sins in life, or I would be condemned to rot in the fires of Hell. I would need more than two lifetimes to make up for all my misdeeds, but I've not got long left of this one, so I have chosen to put right the worse one. That's why I have come to you."

Charlie appraised the puny man and put his knife away.

"Stop this nonsense and tell me what you want with us!" Charlie ordered. "I don't even know you, so how could you have done me any harm?"

The stagehand's reply was as unexpected as it was baffling. "Tell me, Mr Morgan, what's the greatest tragedy that has happened in your life?"

Charlie knew the answer instantly and couldn't help himself. "It was when my father died and the family lost everything. He was shot trying to stop an armed robber. He had no life insurance and we became almost destitute."

"What was the criminal's name?" asked the man in black.

"Legard," said Charlie without hesitation. The name was etched into his memory and would stay with him for as long as he lived. "My mother died of a broken heart." Charlie tried to hold back a tear. "I was young and an only child. I was left with nothing; no home, no money, no parents, so I decided to walk to London to see if I could get a job. I did some labouring for some time and then got an apprenticeship at a vintner's. Eventually I made it work, but it was very hard, I can tell you."

Parr wiped his unpleasant mouth, revealing a severe lack of teeth. "I thought as much," he said. "I knew that would be your answer." He looked about and whispered, "I have information for you, about what really happened."

Charlie Morgan was by now too intrigued to dismiss the stranger. He reasoned that if the man in black intended to harm them he would have done so by now. "Well, go on then," he demanded.

"Legard was a man in trouble. He was an armed robber but he lived a double life because he was associated with well-known and prominent figures. He was in debt because he lived beyond his means. He was approached by a man named Harrison, who happened to be a peer of the realm."

"I know that name," Carolyn said, "but I can't think why."

"Harrison and Legard made a good living out of their partnership. They would identify wealthy targets who they knew did not have life insurance, and Legard would rob them at knife or gunpoint. If a killing happened to occur, then it only made things easier for them. Harrison would move in and purchase their properties and businesses at knock down prices and leave the victim and families destitute. Another scheme was to 'sell' people land or property by illicit means and then take a huge percentage of their profit as he and Legard forced them to sell at the point of a gun, or by other means of blackmail. Whichever scheme they used the result was the same. Actually, that's wrong. They are still in business."

Charlie whispered in horror, "so, my father was a victim of these two."

"Indeed he was," said Parr.

"How do you come to know so much?" Charlie asked.

"Ah, well," said Parr, "that's why I am here. You see I was part of it. I didn't kill your father, but I helped them identify him as a target and set him up for them."

Charlie's blood began to boil and his face reddened with the effort of controlling himself. Parr recognised the signs and for the third time began his next words with an entreaty.

"Please let me explain. I am here to try to make amends. I have carried the guilt ever since and can bear it no longer."

Charlie's memory was flooded by images of his father's body; his mother's terrible wailing grief; the long days afterwards as they declined inexorably into poverty; his mother just giving up the struggle and fading away with a broken heart; his own battle to start life anew in the unforgiving city. He staggered under the weight and Carolyn held on to him as best she could. Yet, despite all that, he found himself unable to harm the pitiful man in black. She studied Parr closely and saw penitence in his face.

"How do I know you are telling me the truth?" he whispered through tightly clenched jaws.

The pathetic stagehand dug deep within a pocket and his hand emerged. He unclenched the tightly balled fist and revealed a gold ring. He placed it in Charlie's outstretched hand.

"It's my father's signet ring," he gasped. "Look Carolyn, can you see his initials?"

"Legard and Harrison gave it to me for my part in the whole thing," Parr admitted sorrowfully. "It's been a millstone round my neck ever since. I was going to fence it, but now I'm glad I kept it, so that it is back with its rightful owner."

"My father was the rightful owner!" muttered Charlie his voice laced with menace. He closed his hand tightly around the ring, leaned against the stone wall beside him and shook with rage and sorrow. A moment later he felt his wife's hand upon his. The fierce pressure with which he gripped the ring subsided.

"We can't stay here any longer," Charlie decided. "You can come with us to the police and we'll sort this out. Let them deal with you and the other two."

"No!" exclaimed Parr, "I didn't come here tonight to set out on a path of revenge. I only want to make amends for my part. I cannot bear it any longer. Besides if you go to the police they will know I've grassed and there will be no hiding place. They'll come after you as well, and your wife."

Charlie studied the stranger in black and made a decision. "I can't forgive you. You'd better disappear and never come back. If I ever see you again, I'll take you to the police myself kicking and screaming if needs be."

He looked again at his father's ring and tears began to well.

"That's fair enough," Parr whispered.

Charlie looked up, but the man in black had backed away into the protection and silence of the dark night. He had disappeared into the maw of the alleyway from whence he had come.

-9-

At the end of each working week Charlie usually found time for a drink or two before making his way home. He was an unusual boss because he encouraged his employees to join him. He wouldn't buy them all a drink every time, of course, and insisted that each person stood his or her corner when the time came.

There were naturally some who couldn't afford to join in, even though they would have liked to, so Charlie quietly, and without anybody else's knowledge, slipped some cash to them when necessary. Those who received his largesse were sworn to silence on pain of dismissal. He preferred to think of it as a sound investment in his staff. Through these acts, and others, he had become a popular boss with a loyal and stable workforce.

On the Friday after the strange encounter with the stagehand, Charlie closed the premises early and made his way to the local pub. As it was only about a quarter of a mile away he left his car and walked. He was accompanied by only two of his senior managers. For some reason nobody else joined them that night. His two managers had been with him for many years and he trusted both. He told them the story that Parr had related to him. They were naturally shocked and began to ask questions, but he brought all conversation to a halt by saying, with a low threatening voice, "I swear I shall kill the men who ruined my family. You know me as a fair man, I hope, but I will not rest until I've seen both buried."

His words stunned his two managers into silence. They had never seen him display such animosity before. They knew him to be a determined character, but this was different and it worried them instantly.

"If you do that, you'll be the first person the police will come for," said one of them.

"I don't think so," replied Charlie. "I think I can find a way to get it done and not be found out."

"You do know that Harrison has friends in high places, don't you?" his other manager asked. "Those sorts of people have contacts everywhere. Corruption is a many headed creature; you can cut off one head and another appears."

"I don't care," Charlie said.

"But, what about your wife?" the first manager asked. "Have you told her?"

"No," Charlie said curtly, "and I don't expect her to hear it from you two either. I will find a way."

Both his managers persisted in their dissuasion.

"What good will it do?"

"What will you gain?"

Charlie's face reflected his steely determination. "It will give me justice. Now, I'll need help from people I can trust. I have told you the situation I'm in, and I've told you what I intend to do about it, so whether you like it or not, you're already involved."

The two senior managers recognised the iron in his words and manner and exchanged glances. They knew he was right; they were now party to the issue and all its ramifications, merely by having been told about it.

"You know you'll be up against people with influence in high places."

It wasn't a question; it was a statement of fact, but Charlie would not be diverted.

"What do we know about Harrison?" he asked his companions. "What makes him tick? What interests does he have?"

"That's simple, boss," said one of his managers.

"He likes other people's money and other men's women, and he has connections that we could only dream about. Also, he has Legard to enforce his wishes."

"I need to know where he lives and what his daily routine is," Charlie was not to be put off.

"He spends most days at The House of Lords.
And either walks to his club near The House or, if the sitting has been late, takes a taxi to his Mayfair apartment." The older of his two managers had already done his homework, but nevertheless tried a final plea. "Please Charlie, as a friend I beg you, don't do this. It will end in tragedy for all of us."

Charlie's response was a sharp glare at them both in turn.

"Harrison will not get away with the death of my father, the death of my mother and the ruination of the family. He will pay. There are consequences to everybody's actions and he will face up to them."

He held up his hand to display the signet ring and the gold caught the light and seemed to burn with all the fury in Charlie's heart.

"OK. You've obviously made up your mind and won't listen to reason. You can rely on our help, and we'll look after Carolyn if it comes to that."

Charlie shook them both by the hand. "Now, let's leave it at that for tonight. I've got some planning to do and I'll let you know what I come up with. It'll be a week or two at least."

For the next two weeks Charlie schemed in his head. He committed nothing to paper or screen for fear of later discovery. He made sure he acted normally and maintained his normal routine. To the outside world it was as if all was as it should be.

Exactly three weeks after he had confided in his two senior managers the usual Friday after work session was in full swing at the nearby pub. Charlie had made sure that at least ten of his employees were present, and two of them had been given their evening's beer money by Charlie, as was his custom. The pub was full. Some people were putting off going home after work, some were killing time before their trains were due, some were beginning a long night on the tiles, some were beginning out of work liaisons and some were meaning to stay for only an hour or so to finish off the week. There was a good humoured, lively buzz in the bar.

The group from Charlie's wine importing company gradually became aware of a disturbance. Another of Charlie's employees had rushed in, hurried to the bar and was using his mobile to call the police. He then moved across to his work colleagues.

"Sorry I'm late. There's a fight down by the river. There's two of them and one's got a knife. There's quite a crowd there already. I've called the police. I just hope they get there in time. It's Charlie; he attacked somebody!"

"Are you ok?" asked a colleague.

"Yes I'm alright, but I think one of them is going to get killed if something's not done. I recognised the other one. It's that Lord Harrison. I've seen him asleep on the telly when they show the House of Lords."

The group rushed out of the pub and ran down to the embankment. They saw Charlie fighting with Lord Harrison, who, despite his age, was almost holding his attacker at bay. There was blood on his hands where he had fended off the knife. Sirens were growing louder and more urgent as the police responded. One car skidded to a halt and four burly officers emerged to assess the scene. One shouted for the men to stop and batons were drawn.

The shout from the uniformed officer caught the attention of Lord Harrison, who looked over towards its source. Charlie saw his opportunity and rushed at him, knocking him backwards against the fence. The wood gave way and Harrison fell to the rocks forty feet below. A family of swans fled as his body rolled down the embankment and into the water. Charlie was quickly handcuffed and shoved roughly into the back of one of the police cars.

One officer climbed down to the water's edge but found no trace of Lord Harrison; the fast flowing current had swept him away. He thought grimly that he would appear at some time much further downstream and wondered just how bloated the body would be by the time he was pulled from the river.

-10-

The Crown Prosecution Service forwarded a sufficiently convincing argument to ensure that the trial took place in camera and reporting restrictions were imposed. The authorities were closing ranks. There was a determination that his murderer be jailed for a long time, preferably life, and that Lord Harrison's name be protected from bad publicity. His affairs and private life were not to be made public. The 'establishment' was a force to be reckoned with, and the ordinary man in the street was powerless against it.

Leading the prosecution case was the county's top barrister, Sir Rex Burnham. He was an arthritic, bald man in his fifties. His rise to prominence was a result of a public school education, an Oxbridge degree, and careful manipulation during his rise to the bar. Sitting in his plush office in London, he reflected that murdering an ass like Harrison was hardly worth the trouble of pursuing. He knew Harrison was a villain, but a well-connected one nonetheless. He realised that the upper echelons of society desperately needed villains like Harrison to save them from their own foolishness and profligacy, so Burnham had been advised to make an example of the vintner, Charlie Morgan.

Rex Burnham knew that it was not that long ago in history that this sort of case would be heard before the Star Chamber rather than in open court. He acknowledged the similarity. He also knew that the Star Chamber did not have the authority to sentence a man to die, but would nevertheless mete out an appropriate punishment. This would probably have been an order that Morgan's ears be hacked off, that he be branded with an iron and transported, banished to the Americas, where he would live as a ruined beggar for the rest of his life. His family would have forfeited whatever estate he had and would have been turned out on the street. The unstated lesson would have been clear: 'do not trouble those who are part of the 'establishment.' Burnham knew that little had changed down the years, but he was not aware of the parallels in Charlie Morgan's life.

Having interviewed each of the significant characters in the case, Sir Rex Burnham left his office and made his way to Southwark Crown Court.

He entered the surprisingly small court room and noted that the number of people permitted to be present was limited, not by the size of the room, but by the case being held in camera. Two burly policemen flanked Charlie Morgan as he was brought into the dock. He was pale and had a bandage covering his temple.

The defence barrister was a man Burnham recognised as a clever advocate and he knew he would be a worthy opponent. Burnham knew that, based on the facts of this case, Morgan could not avoid guilt altogether; rather, the defence would concentrate on mitigating the sentence. His main challenge would be to make sure such a tactic was not successful.

A door opened, and everybody rose on command as the bewigged and robed judge entered. He took his time reaching his place and, before taking his seat, swept the room carefully with a hawkish eye, stressing his status and power. He paid special, lingering attention to the defendant. He then sat slowly and with exaggerated pomposity scanned the court and flicked his robe from under him as he lowered himself. He maintained his silence as he arranged himself and the items before him.

"Proceed."

The charges were intoned loudly for all to hear and Charlie pleaded not guilty in a wavering voice. The judge fixed his gaze on Charlie Morgan.

"The defendant will speak more loudly, for the sake of the record," he instructed. He didn't wait for a reply, preferring instead to hasten events by turning his attention to Sir Rex Burnham.

"We have before us here a clear cut case which should not take up much of our precious time."

His opening sentence was clever because it implied that the court must have more complicated matters to attend to, and that each of the players in the drama could really be spending his or her time more wisely as they were obviously important people whose time was 'precious.'

"The defendant, a vintner named Charlie Morgan, (and that is actually his name rather than Charles), assaulted and murdered Lord Aubrey Harrison on a place known as Temple Wharf. We have witnesses to his unprovoked and violent attack."

Even though the question of whether the attack was or was not 'unprovoked' had yet to be addressed, he was allowed to escape without challenge or rebuke for labelling it as such. Encouraged by the lack of interruption Burnham pressed on and called his first witness. He was duly sworn in and gave his account.

"I was walking to the pub when a man yelled at me that there was a fight down at Temple Wharf. We ran to see what was going on and we found two men fighting. One was that man over there in the dock and he had a knife. The other man was older and he had blood on his hands which must have come from defending himself against the knife."

"Did you hear the men say anything?" asked Burnham.

"Yes. The man with the knife said 'I'll bloody kill you, you bastard." That's all he said. The older man didn't say anything. I think he was out of breath and concentrating on the knife.

"What happened next?"

"A policeman appeared and shouted for the men to stop fighting. The older man looked at him, but the man with the knife just ran at him and the man fell through the railings down into the river."

The defence barrister was given the opportunity to cross examine the witness, but, to everybody's astonishment, declined. The policeman was then called and gave his account, which was exactly the same. Sir Rex Burnham sat himself down and reflected that the case was going well. His satisfaction was cut short, however, when the Defence barrister rose.

"My Lord, I shall let the defendant tell the court what really happened." He sat without further ado as all in court exchanged confused glances.

The prisoner, Charlie Morgan, made his way to the stand and took the oath.

"This is all a horrible mistake. Lord Harrison's death was a tragic accident."

The judge, who viewed it as an open and shut case, could no longer contain himself. "How could it have been a mistake? You attacked the man with a knife and he fell to his death. You may not have stabbed him to death but he assuredly died on the rocks after you forced him through the fence."

"With all due respect," Charlie continued, "I would not have harmed him in any way. We were not fighting; we were practicing."

The entire court drew breath in unison.

The judge intervened again.

"Practicing?"

"Yes, my Lord, I want to be an actor. As you know I own a wine importing company, but I really want to be an actor. I went down there to practice stage fighting in private. Lord Harrison came along, saw what I was doing and offered to help me. He has appeared on stage in the West End at some time in his life, so I took him up on his offer. It was a chance meeting. He even said he might be able to get me a role or two, as he had contacts in the theatre world. I was learning a lot and nothing would have happened if that policemen," he pointed across the court room, "hadn't rushed up and shouted at us just as I was lunging forward. Lord Harrison moved backwards and fell through the fence. I can't tell you how awful it was."

Sir Rex Burnham listened with incredulity. He knew about Lord Harrison's short lived acting career, but had not carried out any research about the defendant. His thoughts were interrupted as Charlie Morgan continued.

"You have heard that I said I'd kill him. That's wrong. Those words were not mine. They were part of the scene I was practicing. My barrister has a sworn statement from a theatre producer to prove that I have been offered a part in a forthcoming drama and it was all a scene from that. I have the script and the directions. It's all in the paperwork. The producer said I had to practice it because we are due to perform live in a few weeks' time."

The judge couldn't hide his disbelief.

"Mr. Morgan, are you serious? You cannot possibly expect this court to believe this. Unless you can produce evidence to support your account, the matter will be ended rapidly."

Charlie Morgan had the temerity to smile at the increasingly irritated judge.

"My Lord, what would you have me do? Would it suffice if the producer of the show appeared before you?"

"It would be a step in the right direction," affirmed the judge.

Charlie nodded to his barrister who turned and signaled to the man that Sir Rex Burnham had earlier thought he recognised. The man who took the stand and the oath was balding, lean and in his late thirties. In answer to questioning he confirmed that he was a theatre producer and that Charlie Morgan was indeed cast to appear in his next show in a few weeks' time.

The judge had to all intents and purposes taken over proceedings, much to the chagrin of the prosecuting barrister.

"Would you tell the court what show it is?"

"Certainly, my Lord. I have been commissioned to stage a scene from a Shakespeare play for the Royal Variety Show. Of course, I have updated it so that it is relevant to a modern audience. It seems the command came from the Palace itself that they wanted something from Othello. As Director of the Royal Shakespeare Company, I thought a modern fight scene would be dramatic."

A hushed murmur went round the court and people shifted in their seats. The judge took it all in and made a decision. The case was now clear. If Charlie Morgan was convicted, the testimony of the Director of the Royal Shakespeare Company would have to be ignored. Her Majesty would undoubtedly become acquainted with that fact and he didn't want to think about the consequences. He knew that there were ways and means by which he could be sanctioned. His career was at stake.

"In the light of what we have heard here today, I am dismissing the charge of murder. I accept the events as described by the defendant. The death of Lord Aubrey Harrison was not intended, which is what is required to satisfy the charge of murder. As there are no lesser charges before me, Mr Morgan, you are free to leave. May I advise you, however, that you would in future be wise to be more careful about where you wield a knife?"

Charlie Morgan bowed his head in gratitude, which masked the smile on his face.

The judge continued," I would like to wish the RSC every success in its production in front of Her Majesty. I hope she enjoys the performance."

Having saved his own bacon, he then cast a stern gaze in the direction of Sir Rex Burnham, who was by this stage looking more than a little sheepish.

"Sir, might I ask that you do your homework more thoroughly in future? A good deal of time and money has been spent on this case and you haven't prepared properly. I shall be discussing the matter elsewhere."

His comments were laced with sarcasm and Burnham was made to feel like a recalcitrant schoolboy.

"My Lord," was all he could manage.

Charlie Morgan, his wife, several employees and the Director of the Royal Shakespeare Company left the court and made their way to their favourite watering hole, not far from the scene of Lord Harrison's demise. The employee who had originally raised the alarm and scurried to the pub sat next to Charlie. He was that year's apprentice. As such, he was not earning much and Charlie often helped him out at the Friday after work drinking sessions. The apprentice for his part had not told a living soul about the arrangement and had been pleased to be able to help his employer. Charlie's investment in his staff had paid off.

LEGARD IN COURT
-11-

It was inevitable that Quentin Legard would appear in court one day. It would have taken a genius to avoid it, considering his criminal history. The problem was that he actually considered himself to be a genius and that arrogance was still in evidence at the meeting. He considered himself invulnerable and untouchable.

"I think you're going to lose this one," he asserted, with total conviction.

"Really; we'll see about that," asserted Sir Rex Burnham, rocking back in his desk chair and studying the man who'd just spoken.

Fifteen years older and forty pounds heavier than Burnham, the defendant Quentin Legard nodded slowly and added, "Definitely. It's very simple; you've got no chance."

His tone was sneering and his voice throaty and rough. The man next to Legard touched his client's arm to restrain him.

"It's ok; he doesn't mind a little sparring," Legard said to his lawyer. "He can take it. Anyway, I'm just telling it like it is."

The defendant unbuttoned his navy suit jacket, blue and rich as an ocean at night; deliberately overt evidence that he considered himself the equal of anybody in the room, whatever their upbringing and social standing. The truth was that Burnham didn't mind sparring at all. The man could say whatever he wanted; Burnham wasn't going to prosecute the case against Legard any more vigorously because of the man's arrogance than he would've held back if the man had been tearful and contrite. On the other hand he wasn't going to get walked on either.

He fixed his eye on Legard's and said in a soft voice, "It's been my experience that what looks pretty clear to one person may turn out to be the opposite. I'm convinced the jury's going to see the facts my way. That means you're going to lose."

It was unusual for the prosecuting and defence teams to meet with the defendant together. Both teams understood the process of plea bargaining and were each well aware of its potential and possible pitfalls.

Sir Rex Burnham had briefed his team before the meeting.

"Plea-bargaining is a process which occurs in relation to criminal offences whereby the offender agrees to plead guilty to a lesser sentence without the need of going through the whole process in the trial to prove that they are in fact guilty. Plea bargaining will most often occur where there is testimony against a co-conspirator or where a lesser charge is offered due to the difficulty of proving the greater charge. It is primarily used by prosecutors to secure the testimony of an individual accused of a crime against a co-conspirator who has been charged with a more serious crime. In many circumstances an individual will be able to negotiate a reduced sentence by pleading guilty to a lesser charge in exchange for agreeing to certain conditions which will often vary depending upon the circumstances of the case. Plea bargaining in this scenario will often occur when the evidence against an individual is overwhelming.

This is regarded as a desirable position by the individual charged with the crime as they will be able to be provided with a lesser sentence as they are charged for the lesser offence to which they pleaded guilty. It is also viewed as a desirable position by the Criminal Justice System as it enables them to sentence a co-conspirator who is more likely to be charged with a much more serious crime. Plea bargains can usually be differentiated into the two following types:

> 1/. A charge plea bargain will enable an accused individual to plead guilty to a lesser crime than the one he is charged with; in most cases falling into one of the two categories outlined above.

> 2/. A sentence plea bargain occurs when a judge informs a defendant of what sentence he will receive if he pleads guilty. It is then up to the defendant to accept or reject the plea bargain.

An individual who has agreed to a plea bargain should ensure with the help of their lawyer that the time and the date when the plea bargain was made are stated on the documents which outline the terms of the deal. The lawyer defending the individual who is the subject of the plea bargain should negotiate and review all the terms of the plea bargain before it is agreed in writing. Reference to the written plea should be made during court proceedings as this will ensure that the existence of the plea bargain will become a matter of court record. Simply mentioning it is enough without the exact terms and conditions stated in the plea bargain being required to be stated in court. Obviously, an individual who is the subject of a plea bargain should always act in accordance with the terms of the plea bargain which will often require testimony in court amongst other things."

Burnham paused to draw breath and assess the state of concentration amongst his team.

"I want you to apply everything I've told you to this particular case. My next point is important. It may well be relevant in this case." He paused again to let the message sink in. "Plea bargains are used in criminal cases, in order to avoid a lengthy trial. The defendant and prosecutor work together to reach an agreement, instead of it going before a jury. It also enables the defendant to prevent the risk of a guilty verdict in court on a more severe sentence. Finally, you should remember that plea-bargaining does not provide benefits to defendants who are innocent."

The session had been the suggestion of the defence team, which Burnham viewed as a tactical error on their part, showing, as it did, either a weakness in their argument or a mistakenly arrogant confidence. Either way, Burnham was pleased to oblige because he reasoned that he may learn something useful. He was, however, aware that the opposition may use the meeting to plant a seed. For their part, the defence team were trying to feed Burnham's already out of control arrogance so that his demise would be all the more painful.

Legard shrugged and looked at his gold Rolex watch. He couldn't have cared less about the time, Burnham suspected. He was simply delivering an aside: that this one piece of jewellery of mine is equal in value to yours, despite your lofty office and place in society, and my lowly position. All a glance at that timepiece would deliver was that this meeting had been a waste of a good half an hour.

In addition to the defendant, his lawyer and Burnham, two other people sat in the office. On Burnham's left was his law clerk, a handsome man in his twenties, Asif Khan, who was a brilliant, meticulous, some said compulsive, worker. He now leaned forward, typing notes and observations about this meeting into his battered laptop. There was a standing joke in the office, hopefully apocryphal, that he took it to bed with him. Certainly, he was inseparable from it. The constant click of the keys drove a lot of people mad, but it had no apparent effect on Legard. The other person in the room was Alicia Tripconey, who had been assigned to Sir Rex Burnham, for the past year. He privately admitted that he would have preferred a younger shadow, but had come to realise that Alicia's maturity had its advantages. She was almost ten years older than him and had become interested in the law late in life after a successful first career raising two teenage boys. Her mind and tongue were as sharp as her confidence was solid. She now looked over Legard's tanned skin, flat stomach, silvery hair, broad shoulders and thick neck.

She then turned to his lawyer and asked, "so, can we assume that this meeting with Mr. Legard and his ego is over with?"

Legard gave a faint, embarrassed laugh, as if a student had said something awkward in class.

The defence lawyer repeated what he'd been saying all along. "My client isn't interested in a deal that involves spending time in jail."

Burnham echoed his own litany. "But that's all we're offering."

"Then he wants to go to trial. He's confident he'll be found innocent."

Sir Rex Burnham couldn't imagine how that was going to happen. He looked long and hard at Quentin Legard, trying to convey his determination that justice for his life of crime was about to be visited upon him. Apart from the matter being discussed that day, the killing of Charlie Morgan's father was still to be resolved. Everybody knew who the killer was, but not enough evidence had yet been unearthed. The unresolved murder stung Burnham, the CPS and the police like a suppurating sore. It may have disappeared from the front pages, but it had not gone away. The matter they were discussing currently was that Quentin Legard had shot a man in the head one Sunday afternoon last March. There was plenty of physical evidence, such as ballistics and gunpowder residue on his hand. There were witnesses who placed him at the scene, searching for the victim just before the death. There were reports of earlier threats by Legard and statements of intent to cause the victim harm. There was a motive. While Sir Rex Burnham was always guarded about the outcomes of the cases he prosecuted, this was as solid as any he'd ever had. He tried one last time, just to make sure that the record reflected his efforts.

"If you accept manslaughter, I'll recommend fifteen years."

"No way," Legard responded, laughing at the absurdity of the suggestion. "You aren't listening are you? I am not going to prison. I'll pay a fine, and it can be as much as you care to make it, I'll do community service, but there will be no jail."

Burnham was normally unflappable, but this man was getting under his skin.

"Mr Legard," he said, addressing him directly rather than speaking through his defence, "you must understand. I am going to prosecute you for premeditated murder. That will carry a life sentence, and in these circumstances, it means exactly what it says on the tin. It is not your prerogative to select a sentence that suits. If you are found guilty, the judge will decide your punishment and in this case it will certainly be a jail sentence. Be in no doubt, I shall be seeking a long period of incarceration."

"What I understand is that I don't see much point in continuing this little get together. You people had better prepare properly this time. I seem to recall you were somewhat embarrassed at the Charlie Morgan trial, Mr Burnham." Legard needled Burnham and it hurt. "You'll have to be better than you were then, if you're going to get me convicted."

"So be it," Burnham stood. He shook the defence lawyer's hand and saw them out. Alicia Tripconey glanced at Legard and his lawyer as if they were clerks who had short-changed her and she remained seated, struggling to keep her thoughts to herself.

When they were gone Burnham sat back in his chair. He spun to look out of the window, and played absently with the only artwork in his office: a baby's mobile of Winnie- the-Pooh characters, stuck to the battered desk with a suction cup. It was his son's, well, had been when the boy was an infant. When he had lost interest in the mobile, his father didn't have the heart to throw it away and brought it here to the office.

He now mused, "I offer him a good deal like that and he says he'll take his chances. The man must be mad. I don't understand it."

Alicia shook her head, "no, it doesn't make sense," she confirmed. "We all know he wouldn't serve his full sentence, probably more like half these days."

Asif Khan supplied the answer. "I know why he won't take what's on offer."

"Enlighten us, o wise one," said Alicia.

"Think about it," said Asif, enjoying the moment. "He can't go to jail."

"Well, nobody wants to go to prison," offered Alicia.

"No, no, I mean he can't. If he goes to prison, whichever one he goes to there are people waiting for him. They're already sharpening spoon handles and grinding down glass, waiting for him. He's crossed so many hardened criminals that he'll be at risk wherever he goes. My bet is that he wouldn't last a week."

"Shame," Alicia declared, as if that was her final word on the subject.

"That's why he killed the victim in this case," continued Asif brightly, warming to his task of enlightening his colleagues. The poor victim had been the sole witness against Legard and Lord Harrison in an extortion case. If Legard had been convicted of that he'd have been jailed for a long time or, apparently, until he was murdered by fellow prisoners."

"That explained the cold-blooded killing, but Legard's reception in prison wasn't high on Burnham's list of priorities. In fact, it wasn't on his list at all. Burnham believed he had a simple task in life and that was to prosecute all who came before him and make sure they got their just deserts. He viewed himself as a protector of the nation's justice system; a knight in shining armour who made sure ordinary citizens could sleep peacefully in their beds at night. To him it was a calling. This attitude was considerably different from many other prosecutors. They took it personally that criminals committed offences, and went after them vindictively, full of rage.

Asif Khan accompanied Alicia Tripconey to her office where they'd spend the evening preparing questions. Burnham himself turned his attention to planning for the trial. He'd carefully studied the facts of the killing. The backbone of the case, the conviction that Burnham wanted most badly was premeditated murder. The sentence for that would be life and it would mean life. Burnham intended to press for that, but it would be a difficult case to prove. He had to establish beyond a reasonable doubt that Legard had planned the victim's demise ahead of time, looked for him, and killed him in circumstances that showed no heat of passion or emotional turmoil. The alternatives were a lesser degree of murder and manslaughter. These were his insurance policies and were easier to prove. If the jury decided, for example, that Legard hadn't planned the murder ahead of time but decided impulsively to kill his victim, he could still be convicted for second-degree murder. He could go to prison for life for this type of murder but he would probably serve less time. Finally, Burnham included the manslaughter charge as a last ditch backup. He'd have to prove only that Legard had killed the man either under conditions of extreme recklessness or in the heat of passion. This would be the easiest of the crimes to prove and on these facts the jury would undoubtedly convict.

That weekend the three prosecutors prepared questions to ask the jury and over the course of the next week they worked hard on preparing their case. Making sure Quentin Legard ended up in jail was nothing more than another brick in the wall of law and order, to which Sir Rex Burnham was so devoted. This particular man's conviction, however, was a very important brick. At various stages in his life Legard had been through court-ordered therapy and though he'd always escaped with a' diagnosis of sanity, the doctors had observed that he was close to being a sociopath; someone for whom human life meant little. He was a bully and petty thug who protected Lord Aubrey Harrison and anybody else who paid him in sufficient quantities. He would intimidate or murder anyone who threatened to testify against him. No one was safe.

"Legard's got money in Europe," Burnham said to his small team.

"I hope he's being watched," said Alicia, "he might just head for the hills."

Legard had been granted bail. The sum involved was close to £1 million, which was almost unheard of, but he had produced it with discomfiting ease. Burnham remembered his assured look not long before as he'd said, "You're going to lose," and wondered if Legard was conveying a subconscious message that he was planning to jump bail.

Asif helped himself to the biscuits that were always available in the office and said, "don't worry, he's got babysitters all over him like a rash. He's wearing a tag, so in theory the police know where he is all the time. I don't think he can do anything without it being known. I like these chocolate ones."

Sir Rex Burnham's prosecuting team, small in number but nevertheless impressive, completed their preparations with total focus. They reminded each other that the victim's family would never see him again and, as an extra incentive, held in the forefront of their minds the image of an arrogant Legard telling them they were going to lose. They considered themselves ready to do battle by the time the jury was selected and sworn in.

-12-

On the morning of the trial, at 9am sharp, he sat down flanked by Alicia Tripconey in her darkest suit, whitest blouse and most assertive visage, and Asif Khan, who was, as usual, manning his battered laptop. Piles of papers, exhibits and law books surrounded them. Across the aisle Quentin Legard sat surrounded by three expensive barristers, two associates and no less than four laptops. The uneven teams didn't bother Burnham at all, however, because he believed he was put on earth to bring people to justice. Some of them would always be richer than you and have better resources. That was how the game worked and Burnham, like every successful prosecutor throughout history, accepted it.

He noticed Quentin Legard staring at him, mouthing something, but he couldn't tell what it was. Alicia helpfully whispered the answer into his ear.

"He says 'you're going to lose'."

Burnham gave a brief laugh. He looked behind him and saw that the court was full. He recognised DCI Sean Mason, who had been after Legard for years and gave a slight nod. The victim's widow returned his gaze with a silent, desperate look that was a plea to bring this terrible man to justice. He tried to convey his confidence to her in his manner and facial expression.

The usher brought the court to order and Burnham felt a chill, even though he had witnessed the opening ritual of the judge's appearance countless times. It was as if a door was closing and shutting out reality as the solemn and mysterious world of the criminal courtroom took over. A few preliminaries were disposed of and the bearded judge nodded for Burnham to begin. He rose and gave his opening statement, which was very short. Sir Rex Burnham could be as long-winded and pompous as any man when the occasion was right, but deep down he believed the divining rod that most effectively pointed toward justice in a criminal case wasn't rhetoric but the truth as revealed by the facts you presented to the jury. Thus for the next two days he produced witness after witness, exhibits, charts and graphs.

"I've been a professional ballistics expert for twenty-two years. I conducted three tests of the bullets taken from the defendant's weapon and I can state without a doubt that the bullet that killed the victim came from the defendant's gun."

"I sold that weapon to the man sitting there, the defendant, Quentin Legard."

"The victim had gone to the police complaining that the defendant had extorted money from him. Yes, that's a copy of the complaint."

"I've been a police officer for seven years. I was one of the first on the scene and I took that particular weapon off the person of the defendant, Quentin Legard."

"We found gunshot residue on the hand of the defendant. The amount and nature of this residue is consistent with what we would've found on the hands of someone who fired a gun about the time the victim was shot."

"The victim was shot once in the temple."

"Yes, I saw the defendant on the day of the shooting. He was walking down the street next to the victim's shop and I heard him stop and ask several people where the defendant was."

"That's correct, sir. I saw the defendant the day the victim was killed. Mr Legard was asking where he could find him. His coat was open and I saw that he had a gun."

"About a month ago I was at a bar. I was sitting next to the defendant and I heard him say he was going to "get" the victim and that'd take care of all his problems."

By introducing all this testimony, Burnham established that Legard had a motive. He'd intended to do it for some time; he went looking for the victim the day he was shot, armed with a gun; he'd behaved with reckless disregard by attacking the man with a gun and firing a shot that could have injured innocent people; and that he in fact was the cause of the victim's death.

One witness stood out from the rest. He delivered his statement from behind a screen so that his identity was protected. He was afforded this facility because he was a former SAS officer. The fact that he had been retired for some time was irrelevant. He had travelled from his home on Exmoor to make his statement and his words were meant to deliver a final, damning, coup de grace. He was there to be a character witness and he described Legard's activities. It did not make for pleasant listening. Murder, extortion, violence, fraud were all laid out in graphic detail and court heard it all in total silence. Not a chair scraped, not a cough was heard. The defence team attempted to stop this happening in the interest of fairness to their client, but it was too late. Quentin Legard listened intently, but gave nothing away. He recognised the voice from behind the screen as belonging to somebody he had met by chance on Exmoor, during the time he had been with a woman named Lisa Richards. She had stabled her horse, on full livery terms, with Ray Quinn's wife. This was prior to Lisa's second attempt at the Golden Horseshoe Challenge, but the arrangement had not ended well.   Quinn did not normally get involved with his wife's business because she was perfectly capable of running it herself, but he had been forced to step in when Lisa Richards' partner, Quentin Legard, had threatened her. Quinn told the court that he "had a word" with Legard and the matter was ended. He was not a man who scared easily, but Ray Quinn having a word had been the most frightening event of his entire life.   Even after some considerable time the recollection still made his heart race and his palms sweat. Ray Quinn had not forgotten the man either, and was only too pleased to be able to assist the court's deliberations. His words had been heard and they carried increased weight due to the fact that he had been a special forces officer.

"Your Honour, the prosecution rests."

He returned to his seat.

"Open and shut," said Asif Khan.

"Shhhh," whispered Alicia Tripconey, "bad luck."

Sir Rex Burnham didn't believe in luck, but he also did not believe in prematurely counting chickens. He sat back and listened to the defence begin its case.

The slickest of Legard's team, the one who'd been in Burnham's office during the ill-fated bargaining session, first introduced into evidence a gun permit which showed that Legard was licensed to own a firearm. Burnham was not disturbed by this because he had known about the licence all along. However, no sooner had the barrister begun to question his first witness, the doorman in Legard's apartment building, than Burnham began to feel uneasy.

"Did you happen to see the defendant on the morning of in question?"

"Yes, I did," the man replied.

Burnham knew that he had obviously been coached to answer the question and not volunteer anything additional. It was a well-known tactic and Burnham would have done the same.

"Did you happen to notice if he was carrying a weapon?"

"I don't know."

Why was he asking this? Burnham asked himself. It would support the prosecution case. He glanced at Alicia who shook her head.

"And did you notice him the day before?"

"Yes."

Burnham was worried. He had an idea where this was headed.

"And did he have his gun with him then?"

"Again, I don't know."

"Where was Mr Legard going when you saw him on those two occasions?"

"He was going into the city. He was trying to get a youth centre up and running, but he was having trouble with gangs and drug dealers who didn't want it. He'd been threatened a lot."

"How do you know?"

"He told me one day and complained that he was not getting enough support from the local authority or the police."

Burnham and Asif Khan exchanged sour glances. The only interest Legard would have in a youth centre was as a venue to sell drugs himself. The defence was trying to paint a picture of an upright citizen attempting to improve things for the youth of the area; a man to be liked and respected for his community work.

"How often did he have a gun with him?" The man returned to his main theme, having scored a point with the jury.

"I've already told you, I don't know. I've worked there for the last three years and I've never noticed anything different about him on any particular day. Anyway, I wouldn't have noticed him carrying a weapon because he would surely have hidden it."

Burnham was convinced the man was lying. Legard must have got to him.

"We've got a problem," whispered Asif Khan.

He meant that if the jury believed Legard always carried a weapon, or indeed that nobody was sure whether he did or did not have it with him at any time, it would undermine Burnham's assertion that he'd taken it with him on that one occasion with the specific intention of murdering the victim. The jury could therefore conclude that he hadn't planned the murder, which would eliminate the premeditation element of the case.

If that witness was a danger to his case, then Burnham was about to be even more deflated by the next one.

"Sir, you don't know the defendant, do you?"

"No, I've never met him or had anything to do with him."

"Has he ever given you anything or offered you any money or anything of value?"

"No, sir."

Burnham instinctively knew he was lying. The witness delivered his lines like a bad actor.

"Now, you heard the prosecution witness say that Mr. Legard was going to quote 'get' the victim and that would take care of all his problems?"

"Yes, I did."

"You were near the defendant and that witness when this conversation supposedly took place, is that right?"

"Yes."

"Where was that?"

"A restaurant, sir."

"And was the conversation the same as the witness has described?"

"No, it wasn't," the man answered the defence lawyer. "The prosecution witness misunderstood. You see, I was sitting at the next table and I heard Mr. Legard say, 'I'm going to get him to take care of some problems I've been having with the gangs. I guess that witness didn't hear it all or something."

"I see," the lawyer summarized in a slick voice. "He was going to get the victim to take care of some problems?"

"Yes, that's it. Mr Legard said that the victim is, sorry was, a good man and I respect him. I'd like him to explain to the community that I'm concerned for their welfare."

Asif Khan mouthed a silent obscenity as the opposition pushed home his point.

"So Mr. Legard was concerned for the welfare of the Local community?"

"Yes he was. Mr. Legard was really patient with him, even though the victim had started all those rumours, you know."

"What rumours?" the lawyer asked.

"About Mr. Legard and the victim's wife."

Behind him Burnham heard the man's widow inhale in shock.

"What were those rumours?"

"For some reason the victim got it into his head that Mr. Legard had been seeing his wife. I know he wasn't, but he was convinced about it. Actually, he thought his wife was seeing a lot of other men. I think he was obsessed."

Sir Rex Burnham could not let it continue unopposed.

"Objection," he snapped.

"Let me rephrase, then. What did the victim ever say to you about Mr Legard and his wife?"

"He said he was going to get even with Legard because of the affair; sorry, I mean the supposed affair."

Burnham glanced at the face of the victim's widow, shaking her head slowly with tears running down her cheeks as the defence lawyer decided to finish. Sir Rex did his best to punch holes in the man's story. He thought he did a pretty good job. The problem was that much of the testimony had been speculation and opinion, such as the rumour of the affair, and there was little he could do to discredit him. He returned to his chair. Relax, Burnham told himself as he put down the pen he'd been playing with compulsively. The lesser murder charge was still alive and undamaged. All the jury would have to do was to find that Legard had killed his victim, albeit at the last minute, and Burnham believed he had already dealt with that successfully.

-13-

The defence lawyer called another witness. His name was Winston Albright. He was a slightly rotund grandfatherly sort of man with a friendly face and he described himself as a good friend of the defendant. Burnham thought about this and concluded that any concerns the jury may have about Albright's potential bias were outweighed by the fact that the suspect, it seemed, had 'good friends' in the community. Burnham knew that to be a complete lie, because he believed Legard saw his local community not as friends but only as golden opportunities for his extortion and loan sharking operations. His thoughts were interrupted as the defence began anew.

"Now you heard the prosecution witness say that Mr. Legard went looking for the victim on the day of the tragic shooting?"

"Tragic? He's making it sound like a complete accident," Khan was whispering again.

"Yes." The witness answered the lawyer's question.

"Can you confirm that Mr.Legard went looking for the victim on the day of the shooting?"

"Yes that's right. He did go looking for him."

Sir Rex Burnham leaned forward and wondered where this was going.

"Could you explain what happened and what you saw?"

"Of course; I'd been in church with Mr. Legard."

"Excuse me," the lawyer said, "church?"

"Yes, we went to the same church. I have to admit though that he went more than me. He went at least twice a week; sometimes three."

"O Lord!" an exasperated Alicia Tripconey said, without realising the irony.

Burnham counted four crucifixes hanging from the necks of the jury, and not a single eyebrow among those men and women rose in irony at this gratuitous mention of the defence witness's piety, or that of Legard.

"Please go on, Mr. Albright."

"And I stopped at the coffee shop with Mr. Legard and we got some coffee and sat outside. Then he asked a couple of people if they'd seen the victim, because he went there a lot."

"Do you know why the defendant wanted to see the victim?"

"He wanted to give him this game he bought for his son."

"What?" the widow behind Burnham whispered in shock. "No, no, no ...."

"A present, you know. Mr. Legard loves children and he wanted to give it to the victim for his boy."

"Why did he want to give him a present?"

Albright replied, "he said he wanted to patch things up with the victim. He felt uncomfortable. He was worried that the boy would hear the rumours and think they were true. He thought a present for the boy would break the ice. Then he was going to talk to the victim and try to convince him that he was wrong."

"Keep going, sir. What happened next?"

"Then Mr. Legard saw the victim outside his shop and went to talk to him."

"And then?"

"He started to give him the bag but the victim just pushed it away and started yelling at him."

"Do you know what they were yelling about?"

"The victim was convinced the rumours were true and was shouting things like. 'I know you've been seeing my wife for years.' I don't think that could be true because they had only moved here last year."

"No, no!" the widow cried. "It's all a lie!"

The judge banged his gavel dawn, though it was with a lethargy that suggested his sympathies were with the woman. Burnham sighed in disgust. He knew the defence had introduced a motive suggesting that the victim, not Legard, might have been the aggressive one in the fight that day.

"I know it wasn't true," the witness said, determined to complete his offering. "Mr Legard would never do anything like that. He was really religious."

Sir Rex Burnham rolled his eyes heavenward as he recognised the implication that Mr Quentin Legard was a saint rather than a sinner.

The lawyer then asked, "did you see what happened?"

"It was all kind of blur, but I saw the victim grab something like a metal pipe or a piece of wood and take a swing at Mr Legard. He tried to back away, but there was nowhere for him to go. They were in an alley. Finally, it looked like he was going to get his head smashed and Mr Legard pulled out a gun. I think he was just trying to scare the victim; to stop the attack."

"Objection; the witness couldn't have known what the defendant's intentions were."

The lawyer asked the witness, "What, Mr. Albright, was your impression about Mr Legard's intentions?"

"It looked like he was just going to threaten him, but the man swung at him a few more times with the pipe. Mr Legard still didn't shoot. Then the victim grabbed his arm and they were struggling for the gun. Mr Legard was yelling for people to get down and shouting for the victim to let go before somebody got hurt."

Burnham knew the events were being portrayed as something other than the reckless behaviour or heat of passion that it was necessary to show to prove manslaughter. He had a sinking feeling in the pit of his stomach.

"Mr. Legard was pretty brave. I mean, he could have saved himself but he was worried about bystanders. He was always worrying about other people, especially children."

Burnham wondered who had written the script.

"Then I ducked because I thought that if the victim managed to get the gun he'd just start shooting like a mad man. I admit I was scared. I heard a gunshot and when I got up off the ground I saw that the victim was dead."

"What was the defendant doing?"

"He was on his knees, trying to help the victim. It looked like he was trying to stop the bleeding. He was shaking and calling for help."

"No further questions."

The witness was handed over to Burnham. He tried to puncture Albright's testimony, but because it had been cleverly phrased he knew the damage had been done. He planted a seed of doubt in the minds of the jury by asking again, several times, if Legard had paid the witness anything or threatened his family, but the man denied it.

The defence then called a doctor whose testimony was short and to the point; almost surgical.

"Doctor, the coroner's report shows the victim was shot once in the side of the head. Yet you heard the testimony of the previous witness that the two men were struggling face to face. How could the victim have been shot in that way?"

"A shot in the side of the head would be consistent with the victim turning his head away from the weapon while he was exerting pressure on the trigger, hoping to hit Mr Legard."

"So in effect you're saying that the victim shot himself."

Burnham leapt to his feet, "objection."

The judge warned the defence, who merely shrugged his shoulders and pressed on.

"You're saying that it's possible the victim was turning away while he himself pulled the trigger of the weapon, resulting in his own death?"

"That's correct."

"No further questions."

Burnham was slower to his feet this time. He asked the doctor how it was that the coroner hadn't found any gunshot residue on the victim's hands, which would have been present if he'd fired the gun himself, while Mr Legard's had residue on them. The doctor thought the answer was obvious and showed his impatience at what he saw as Burnham's lack of understanding and intellectual prowess. He sighed before explaining that Mr Legard's hands were covering those of the victim so they got the residue on them. The judge dismissed the witness and Burnham returned to his place with a glance at the stony face of the defendant who was staring back at him.

Burnham heard the words 'you're going to lose' playing back in his head and shifted uncomfortably. He hadn't thought it was a possibility before the case began, but was now less sure. There was an increasing chance that Legard would walk away.

Then the defence lawyer called his final witness: Quentin Legard himself. His testimony gave a story identical to that of the other witnesses and supported his case: that nobody could be sure whether he normally had a gun with him, that the victim had this strange idea about Legard and his wife, that he'd never used extortion in his life, that he bought a present for the victim's son, that he wanted to enlist his help in putting money into the local community, that the struggle occurred just as the witness said. For extra effect he added that he had given the victim mouth-to-mouth resuscitation. Finally he commented that he wanted to help minorities in the community and he felt the police and local politicians don't like it. He bowed his head and looked sorrowfully at the floor as he went on to say that he had accidently hurt one of the very people he was attempting to help. It was, to say the least, an effective performance.

Alicia Tripconey's sigh could be heard throughout the courtroom and drew a glare from the judge.

"What do we do now?" Asif Khan asked quietly.

Burnham glanced at the two people on his team who'd worked so tirelessly, for endless hours, on this case. He then looked into the eyes of the victim's wife, whose life had been so terribly altered by the man sitting on the witness stand, gazing placidly at the prosecutors and the people in the public gallery. He pulled Khan's laptop closer to him and scrolled through the notes that the young man had taken during the course of the trial. He read for a moment then stood slowly and walked toward Legard.

In his trademark polite voice he asked, "Mr. Legard, I'm curious about one thing."

"Yes sir?" the killer asked, just as politely. He'd been coached well by his team who had undoubtedly urged him never to get flustered or angry on the stand.

"The game you got for the victim's son."

The eyes flickered. "Yes? What about it?"

"What was it?"

"One of those little computer games."

"Was it expensive?"

A smile of curiosity passed across Legard's face. "Yes, it was fairly expensive, but I wanted to do something nice for him and his son. I felt bad because his father was pretty crazy..."

"Just answer the question," Burnham interrupted.

"It cost about two hundred pounds."

"Where did you get it?"

"A shop in the shopping centre, I can't remember the name."

"What time was that?"

"About ten thirty or so, I was on the way to the eleven o'clock service."

Burnham then asked, "at which church?"

"St John's."

"Did you go straight there, with the game in your pocket?"

"Yes, obviously." Legard's sneer was plain for all to see.

"So the game was with you in the church?"

"Obviously," replied Legard, correcting his facial expression into what he hoped would be seen as a helpful smile.

"But nobody would have seen it because it was in your pocket?"

"Obviously," Legard responded, unable to stop himself from using the annoying word for the third time. He tried to remain polite and unflustered.

"When you left the church did you walk along the high street to the coffee shop in the company of the earlier witness, Mr Winston Albright?"

"Yes, that's right."

"Was the game still in your pocket?"

"No."

"Why not?"

"At that point I took it out and was carrying it in the bag."

Burnham whirled round and asked in a piercing voice, "isn't it true that you didn't have the game with you in church?"

"No," Legard said, blinking in surprise but keeping his voice even and low, "that's not true at all. I had the game with me all day, until I was attacked by the victim."

"Isn't it true that you left church, returned home, got the game and then drove to the coffee shop?"

"No, I wouldn't have had time to go home after church and get the game. The service finished at midday and I got to the coffee shop about ten minutes later. I told you, I live a good twenty minutes from the church. You can check a map. I went straight from St. John's to the coffee shop."

Burnham looked away from Legard to the faces of the jury. He then glanced at the widow in the front row. Burnham considered himself to be a pretty good lie detector and he could see that Legard was making it all up. He'd probably seen an advert for that game on that same morning, but he doubted the jury would realise. To them he was simply co-operating and politely answering the prosecutor's somewhat curious questions.

"What did this game do?"

"Objection," the lawyer called. "What's the point?"

"Your honour," Burnham said. "I'm just trying to establish a relationship between the defendant and the victim."

"Go ahead, Mr. Burnham, but I don't think we need to know what kind of box this toy came in."

"Actually, I was going to ask that."

"Well, don't.

"I won't. Now, Mr. Legard, what did this game do?"

"I don't know, you shot spaceships or had a battle or something."

"Did you play with it before giving it to the victim?"

From the corner of his eye he saw Alicia and Asif exchange troubled glances, wondering what on earth their leader was up to.

"No," Legard answered. For the first time he seemed uncomfortable. "I don't like games. Anyway, it was a present. I wasn't going to open it before I gave it to the boy."

Burnham nodded, raised an eyebrow and continued his questioning.

"Now did you have the game with you when you left your house on the morning of the day the victim was shot?"

"Yes, I did."

"Was it in a bag?"

He thought for a moment. "Yes, but I put it in my pocket. It wasn't that big."

"So your hands would be free?"

"Well, yes, probably."

Somebody in the public gallery was crying softly and the faces of his prosecution team reflected their confusion. He saw people glancing at one another. Everybody was waiting for him to drop a brilliant bombshell that would destroy Legard's testimony and expose him as the liar and killer that he was.

Burnham took a deep breath and said, "I have no further questions."

There was a moment of silence. Even the judge frowned and seemed to want to ask if the prosecutor was sure he wanted to do this. But he settled for asking the defence lawyer, "Have you any more witnesses?"

"No, sir; the defence rests."

-14-

The sole reason for a jury's existence is that people lie. If everyone told the truth a judge could simply ask Quentin Legard if he planned and carried out the murder and the man would say yes or no and that would be that. But people don't tell the truth, of course, and so the judicial system relies on a jury to look at the eyes and mouths and hands and postures of witnesses and listen to their words and decide what the truth is and what it isn't. The jury in this particular case had been out for two hours. Burnham and his assistants were holed up in the cafeteria in the building across from the court. Nobody was saying a word. Some of this silence had to be attributed to their uneasiness, if not outright embarrassment, at Burnham's unfathomable line of questioning about the game Legard had allegedly bought for the victim's son. They would probably be thinking that even experienced prosecutors get flustered and fumble the ball from time to time and it was just as well it happened during a case like this, which was, apparently, unwinnable.

Sir Rex Burnham's eyes were closed as he lounged back in an ugly orange plastic chair. He was replaying Legard's demeanour and the witnesses' claims that they hadn't been threatened or bribed by Legard. He knew they had all been paid or threatened or both, but he had to admit they looked and sounded fairly credible to him and so presumably they would seem that way to the jury as well. However, Burnham had learned to have great respect for the jury system and for jurors on the whole and, as they met in the small deliberation room they might easily be concluding at this moment that Legard had bullied and coerced the witnesses into lying as well and that he was therefore guilty of murder. He opened his eyes and glanced over at Alicia Tripconey and Asif Khan and their discouraged faces told him that there was also a pretty good chance that justice might not get done this time.

"Ok," Alicia said, "so we don't win on premeditated murder. We've still got the two lesser charges. They'll have to convict on manslaughter."

"Have to?" thought Burnham. He didn't think that was a phrase that ever applied to a jury's decision. The defence had pitched a great case for a purely accidental death.

"Miracles happen," said Khan, with youthful enthusiasm.

And that was when Burnham's mobile rang. It was the clerk with the news that the jury was returning.

"That's fast, is that good or bad?" Khan asked.

"You can never tell," said Burnham. "Let's find out."

He left his coffee to get cold.

"Ladies and gentlemen of the jury, have you reached a verdict?"

"We have, your Honour."

The foreman, a middle-aged man in a blue cotton shirt and dark trousers held out a piece of paper, which was transferred to the judge. Burnham's kept his eyes locked onto Legard's, but the killer was sitting in his chair examining his manicured hands with a placid expression. If he was worried about the outcome of the trial he wasn't showing it. The judge read the slip of paper silently and glanced over at the jury. Burnham tried to read the expressions on the faces of the individual jurors but couldn't.

"The defendant will stand." The order boomed into the corners of the court, and Legard and his lawyer stood.

The judge handed the paper to the clerk.

"On the charge of premeditated murder the jury finds the defendant not guilty. On the second charge of murder the jury finds the defendant not guilty. On the third charge of manslaughter the jury finds the defendant not guilty."

The entire room was totally silent for a brief moment as the words sunk in. Then Legard let out a yelp of delight and raised his clenched fist into the air in his moment of victory. The judge, clearly disgusted at the verdict, banged his gavel and warned Mr Legard as to his behaviour.

"See the clerk for the return of your passport and bail deposit." Then, as a gruff concluding addition, said, "I only hope that if you're brought up on charges again you appear in my court." He ended with another angry slap of his gavel.

The room broke into a hundred simultaneous conversations after the judge had swept out with an annoyed twirl of his robe wearing a thunderous face. Legard ignored the commotion and shook hands with his team and supporters. Several of his confederates came up to him and gave him hugs. Burnham saw a smile pass between Legard and Albright. The prosecutor shook hands with his team, as he always did at the end of a case, and made his way to the crying widow. He hugged her.

"I'm sorry," he said.

"You did your best," the woman said and patted at the tears running down her cheeks. "I suppose people like that, really bad people, don't play by the rules. There's nothing you can do about it; they're just going to win."

"Next time," Burnham said."

"Next time," she whispered cynically, not believing in justice any more.

Sir Rex Burnham noticed Legard walking toward the front door of the court and turned to whisper a few words to the nearby policeman. Legard did not notice the brief exchange.

"Nice try, Mr Burnham," the jubilant man said, "but I told you that you were going to lose. You should have listened."

One of his lawyers handed Legard an envelope. He opened it and took out his passport.

"It must have cost you a lot to bribe those witnesses," Burnham said amiably.

"Oh, I wouldn't do that," Legard frowned, "that would be a crime, as you of all people should know."

Alicia Tripconey pointed a finger at him and said, "you're going to make a mistake and we're going to be there when it happens."

Legard replied calmly, "only if you're moving to the south of France, which is where I'm going next week. Why don't you all come over and get some sunshine?" He mocked and turned to the door.

"Mr Legard," Burnham said, "one more thing."

The killer turned as Burnham nodded to the policeman. Legard was stopped in his tracks by a large figure blocking his exit.

"Is there something you want?" he asked.

The answer was not made with words, but with a pair of handcuffs being snapped smartly around his wrists. Winston Albright and a couple of Legard's minders stepped forward but they too were halted by other burly officers. They backed away instantly.

"Hey, what the hell's going on?" Legard shouted as his lawyer pushed his way forward.

"What's happening here?" he demanded.

The suited policeman ignored him.

"Quentin Legard you are under arrest for unlawful possession of a firearm in a public place." The officer intoned the rest of the litany as people in the vicinity shuffled away trying to distance themselves, as if contagion was in the air.

Legard snapped at his lawyer. "Why the hell are you letting him do this? I'm paying you; do something!"

This attitude didn't sit well with the lawyer but he said, "He's been acquitted of all charges."

"Actually not all charges," Burnham said, "there was one lesser offence I didn't bring him up on. Following the Dunblane massacre the government passed the Firearms (Amendment) Act 1997 and the Firearms (Amendment) (No 2) Act 1997,banning private possession of handguns almost completely. Exceptions to the ban include muzzle-loading "black powder" guns, pistols produced before 1917, pistols of historical interest (such as pistols used in notable crimes, rare prototypes, unusual serial numbers and so on), starting pistols, pistols that are of particular aesthetic interest (such as engraved or jewelled guns) and shot pistols for pest control. Under certain circumstances, individuals may be issued a PPW (Personal Protection Weapon) licence. Even the UK's Olympic shooters fall under this ban. Shooters can only train in Northern Ireland, the Channel Islands, the Isle of Man or abroad, which means Switzerland in real terms.

"What the hell is that?" Legard snapped again.

His lawyer shook his head. "I don't know," was all he could muster.

"You're my lawyer, what do you mean, you don't know?"

Burnham said, "it's a law that makes it an offence to have a loaded firearm in a public place."

Legard said, "you can't do that; it's too late, the trial is over."

The lawyer said, "he can, Quentin, it's a different charge."

"Well, he can't prove it," Legard snapped. "Nobody saw any guns; there were no witnesses."

"As a matter of fact there is a witness, and he happens to be one you can't bribe or threaten."

"Who?"

"You."

Burnham walked to the computer on which Asif Khan had transcribed much of the testimony. He read aloud. "No, I wouldn't have had time to go home after church and get the game. The service finished at midday and I got to the coffee shop about ten minutes later. I told you my house is a good twenty minutes away from the church. You can check a map. I went straight from St. John's to the coffee shop."

"What's this all about?" Legard demanded. "What's the problem about the game?"

"The game's irrelevant," Burnham explained, "what's important is that you said you didn't have time to go home between leaving the church and arriving at the coffee shop. That means you had to have the gun with you in church and in other public places. You admitted under oath that you broke the law. The transcript is admissible at your next trial. That means it's virtually an automatic conviction."

Legard swallowed his rising anger and hissed, "Ok, let me pay the fine and get the hell out of here. I'll do it now."

Burnham looked at his lawyer. "Do you want to tell him or shall I?"

His lawyer shook his head. "It means a mandatory jail sentence. The government passed the law in response to public pressure."

"What?" Terror blossomed in the killer's eyes. "But I can't go to prison." He turned to his lawyer, grabbing his arm. "I told you that. They'll kill me in there. I can't. Do something; earn your money for a change."

Legard was becoming increasingly desperate and gripped his arm.

The lawyer pulled the man's hand off. "You know what, Quentin? Why don't you tell your story to your new lawyer? I'm in the market for a better grade of client." The man turned and walked out through the swinging doors.

"Wait!"

Legard was escorted firmly away, shouting his protests. After some congratulations from police officers and spectators, Burnham and his team returned to their table and began organizing books and papers and laptops. There was a huge amount of material to pack up; the law, after all, is nothing more or less than words.

"Well, you got him," Asif Khan said. "You made him focus on the game and he didn't think about the gun."

"We thought you'd lost the plot," put in Alicia Tripconey, admiration in her eyes. "Let's have a drink to celebrate."

The arthritic, balding Sir Rex Burnham declined. He was desperate to get home and spend more time with his long suffering wife and their weakening wheelchair bound son. He packed the big bags quickly.

"Thank you," a woman's voice said.

Burnham turned to see the victim's widow standing in front of him. He nodded. She seemed to be casting about for something else to say but then she just shook the prosecutor's hand and she and an older woman walked out of the nearly empty courtroom. Burnham watched her leave.

"I suppose people like that, really bad people, don't play by the rules and there's nothing you can do about it. Sometimes they're just going to win, but that means sometimes they're not," he muttered under his breath, as he hefted the largest of the litigation bags and together the three prosecutors left the courtroom.

Having concentrated intently throughout the proceedings from his front seat in the public gallery, the last person to exit the court smiled to himself. Charlie Morgan nodded towards the milling crowd below and walked quietly into the gathering darkness of the evening. He didn't know that he had also seen the receding figure of Ray Quinn, who was in a hurry to return to his wife and his quiet life on Exmoor.

The judge had not long left the courtroom before he was told that it was he who would be taking the case.

He was a diligent man and soon found the precedent he sought. It was actually pointed out to him by Sir Rex Burnham, but the judge was not above allowing the plaudits to come his way. Legard's lawyer would argue vehemently against a custodial sentence, but he would be fighting a losing battle.

Not far away, in the prison to which Legard was due to be sent, inmates were already sharpening spoon handles and fashioning stilettos from spare pieces of glass. Even the unofficial bookmakers within the jail were no longer taking bets about how long he would last. It was a foregone conclusion. The betting had already turned to concentrating on who would do it.

QUINN MAKES PLANS
-15-

It was generally assumed that Ray Quinn was returning immediately to Exmoor and his quiet life. In fact, he had no intention of doing so. He had arranged to spend an evening in London with old friends and catch the last train from Paddington. He had plenty to talk about.

Over dinner at a quiet hotel, far from anybody's hearing, he held John Lomax and Leanne in captivated silence. Also present was the man who had acted as their 'minder' after Quinn had departed for his new life on Exmoor. Frank had encountered no problems fulfilling his role and was enjoying living in the city and experiencing all its facilities. That was about to change.

Ray Quinn was in business mode.

"Frank, how would you like to become a member of the clergy?"

"You must be joking!"

"I never joke about business, you of all people know that."

Frank was stunned. "Oh Lord, I have a funny feeling about this."

"I can't do it," said Quinn, smiling at his friend's discomfort and unintended reference. "My voice would be recognised and my target must not be aware of what is happening. He doesn't know you. In fact, he's never met you or heard your voice. Also, you think like me. Most importantly, I know I can trust you to get the job done."

Frank was intrigued. "Tell me, then."

"I want you to be a Prison Chaplain. I'll arrange all the necessary background and paperwork. Our friends will sort that out for us. As soon as I know which prison, I'll let you know."

"And just what do you want me to do while I'm there? I've not got any experience of being a priest, believe it or not."

"You'll manage," said Quinn.

Frank recognised the signs. He knew there would be no point arguing. In this mood, Ray Quinn was not a man to be denied. "I bet you've already got all the arrangements sorted."

Quinn laughed. "Of course. You wouldn't expect anything else, would you?" He pulled a large brown envelope from his overnight bag and pushed it across the table. "It's all in there. Just follow and be a good man. Oh, by the way, your name will be Father Luke. He's a teacher, you know. Rather fitting, I think, as we're going to teach somebody a lesson. This has been cleared at the highest level, so you won't have any problems from that side of things."

John Lomax and Leanne witnessed the exchange with amusement.

"You said, 'we,'" noted Lomax, looking at his old friend.

"I see you're as sharp as ever," mocked Quinn, "despite your age!"

"Well?" asked Leanne. She knew that whatever was being planned would be serious. She also knew it would be enormous fun along the way.

"Ah, you two. I need you two to be husband and wife tourists. Slipping serenely towards your pensions and taking trips that you've always promised yourselves." He pushed a slimmer envelope towards Lomax. "Read and digest. You'll enjoy it."

"Mysterious," said Leanne.

That would prove to be the understatement of all time.

"I'm sorry about the interruption to your everyday routines, but I need you to do this. You see, the target upset my wife and you know how I feel about that. I cannot leave that unremarked."

Lomax, Leanne and Frank immediately understood and felt sorry for their target, whoever he was. It was not a good idea to cross Ray Quinn. Worse still, it was not a good idea to upset his wife. He took that rather personally.

Dinner ended and Quinn set out to catch his train, content with the arrangements he had put in place. He set the alarm on his watch to wake him half an hour before his destination and settled comfortably in his first class seat. He dozed with a confident calm and went over what was to come.

LEGARD GETS RELIGION
-16-

Legard's fight against a custodial sentence collapsed quickly. He was refused bail for two reasons. The judge believed he would disappear and he also considered him to be a considerable danger to the public. He was placed in isolation for his own safety whilst awaiting sentence. He inevitably lost his battle and was given fifteen years.

Being alone was not a problem for him. He had survived much in his life already, largely because he had developed coping strategies. These now proved useful. He was not in the least afraid of physical harm. He knew that fellow inmates would seize any opportunity to use their sharpened spoon handles and home-made stilettos and he was ever watchful. He also knew that the prison staff could not be trusted either, because it only took one of them to succumb to a bribe and he would be in mortal danger.

"Let me introduce myself. My name is Father Luke, but you may call me Luke. Like you, I'm new to this place, so we'll learn together. I am part of the team of Prison Chaplains, but, more importantly, I have been assigned specifically to you. I've been told you're in need of special care."

Quentin Legard realised very early in his sentence that the only regular human contact that was possible in his particular situation would be with a Prison Chaplain. He therefore adopted a practical approach, and accepted his new mentor at face value. For his part, Frank, or Luke as he had become, set about learning as much as he could about his unaccustomed role. He immersed himself in the material that Quinn had provided, whilst Legard immersed himself in whatever literature was available, but at the same time read other materials copiously to deflect suspicion. He was trying to show the prison staff that he recognised the error of his ways and was a changed man. He was showing the authorities that they could, and should, trust him. He knew he had to put his trust in the Prison Chaplain, who had arrived at much the same time as him. He had given his name as Luke and he seemed to take a particular interest in Quentin. He regarded it as suspicious, but was in no position to argue. He resolved to go along with it and hope that his situation might change for the better.

Quentin Legard had no choice. He listened with as much politeness as he could muster to Luke.

"If we are to work together, you need to understand my precise role with you. I am not your normal, run of the mill Prison Chaplain, but I expect you've already realised that."

Legard did not respond. He didn't want, at this stage, to give away anything at all.

"The first job of a Prison Chaplain is what is known as a 'reception visit.' Each new prisoner is visited within a day of arrival. Sadly, in some cases, it's just a 'hello again, welcome back' to a recalcitrant convict. They get a chaplaincy leaflet and that's that. But for some people that visit is immensely important. The newly convicted inmate may have just received a long sentence and will be reeling from the turn of events. He may be resentful, angry and perhaps violent."

"Please be assured I am not a violent man," said Quentin.

"Fine. Thank you," Luke continued. "I'll come to work each morning with the rest of the staff. I'll be searched. Even Prison Chaplains have been known to smuggle things like mobile phones. If a prisoner's relative dies, I'll have to break the bad news. I don't think that will happen to you, but it may."

"In other words, I'm being treated as a special case." Quentin was perceptive.

"Indeed you are," confirmed Luke. "You have me as your personal clergyman. Oh, by the way, if you feel the need to pray, I can arrange a time when you could go to chapel and light a candle and pray."

Legard sniffed. He didn't think he would be needing such an advantage.

Luke ploughed on. "I need you to listen and understand exactly what I'm telling you. The arrangements for you are unique. In return, I have to insist we trust each other, no matter what happens. I shall not tell any prison staff anything you tell me. That's important. Confidence is going to be vital for you."

"What are you saying?" Legard was puzzled. "I get the impression you're saying there's a chance you could help me get out of here."

"Don't jump the gun," Luke commanded. "Let things happen in a natural way. You have plenty of time."

"You're not wrong there!" Legard said, surprised that a clergyman would be so unfeeling.

"Let's move on," suggested Luke. "Is there anybody who is likely to visit you?"

"No."

The brevity of Legard's answer took Luke aback.

"I trust you're not on drugs," continued Luke.

"Never! I hate anything to do with them and the people who supply them are scum."

"Amen to that." Luke was living the role.

"Do you play chess?" asked Legard.

"As a matter of fact, I do," Luke replied. "Perhaps we'll spend some time across a chessboard. Friendly battle, of course."

"Naturally," confirmed Legard.

"I think I'd like to pray," said Luke.

"What? Here? Now?! Asked Legard.

"Certainly," Luke responded. "Prayer is not confined to particular times or places, as far as I am concerned. Actually, I think the present situation is fitting. Yes, Quentin, let me help you begin your journey."

Legard was confused. Why should this man believe he could change him? What gave him the right to try? Such arrogance! He verbalised these thoughts in a toned down way.

"I have to tell you that I'm not religious; never have been. I'm not sure I even believe all that stuff, if you'll pardon me saying so."

"That's no problem. We all start somewhere. Nobody is a totally lost cause. You'll find God never abandons you. I can help you. It's what I've been called to do."

Legard noted that Luke was speaking as if he were reeling off bullet points from a script.

"Sit with me, Quentin. I'll pray for you here and now. You don't have to do anything except be calm and still for a while. Can you do that?" asked Luke.

"I suppose so," Legard acceded grudgingly.

And so Luke prayed for Quentin Legard there and then, in that small cell. Legard noticed that the usual noises of prison life ceased for the five minutes it took. It was as if a blanket of calm and peace had settled over that dark and violent place. Luke finished by asking for forgiveness for the man in his charge. He slowly uncoupled his fingers and rested his hands on the table between them.

"I think that will be enough for today," said Luke. "I hope you have a peaceful night. I'll see you at the same time tomorrow. We can play chess again, if you like. We don't have to pray every day we meet, but I would like to, if that's all right. I think it might help you, given your situation."

Quentin Legard, the man of violence and a convicted criminal, shrugged his shoulders. It was no skin off his nose if this strange man wanted to pray for him. Who was he to stop him? If it made him feel better, then let him get on with it. Besides, he got a game of chess and some safe adult contact out of it, so it seemed a fair exchange.

Hours turned into days; days became weeks and weeks begat months as Quentin Legard settled into a routine. He considered it agreeable enough given the circumstances, but Luke was aware of a growing tension.

"I'd like to pray," Legard announced suddenly during a game of chess.

Luke masked his surprise well.

"Good idea. You need all the help you can get," said Luke. "I'm just about to beat you."

"No way. I'll finish you off first, then you can help me pray."

The remainder of the game was played in silence and the time between moves became longer each time. On the surface, to anybody watching, they were contemplating moves. Not that anybody was around to witness the game. Each man, however, was thinking deeply about other things. The chess match was a front.

Luke was turning his mind to Legard's sudden need for prayer. He was well aware that it was not a genuine cry from the heart. He knew that the prisoner had to find a way to persuade authority that he was a changed man, or at least a man on the road to redemption. He understood that the only way that could happen would be if he could convince Luke. Unfortunately for Legard, Luke was not such an easy touch. He had witnessed such false confession when serving in the SAS with Ray Quinn. He recalled one unfortunate would be terrorist who had offered the names and locations of his fellow fighters. He and Quinn had quietly and efficiently extracted the information and then calmly, without compunction, terminated him for his own sake. By comparison, Quentin Legard was a mere schoolboy and his attempt at forgiveness was, in his view, pathetic and pitiful.

For his part, Legard had already come to rely on this strange priest. He had given his name as Luke, but Legard was not naïve enough to believe that. He had many questions about the man and felt he had nothing to lose by asking them.

"Luke," he began, "I don't believe you are really a priest. If I'm going to be here for a long time, and we are to spend so much time together, I think we should be honest with each other."

He was fishing.

Luke's reply startled him. "I agree," he said, as he raised his eyes to cast his gaze upon Legard's expectant face.

Luke allowed the silence to grow. He wanted the other man to begin and he held his gaze. Legard became uncomfortable under the scrutiny.

"Well, I've got all the time in the world. You start," said Legard, trying to lead and therefore control the situation.

Luke recognised what was being tried and smiled. He was in total control and could afford to allow his man to believe it was the other way round. Legard took the smile to mean acquiescence.

"Where to begin?" mused Luke.

"How about the beginning?" Quentin could not resist the opportunity for sarcasm.

Luke favoured him with another tolerant smile.

"Well, although you don't believe it, I am actually a priest. A proper, fully grown-up minister. I don't preach in any particular church, though. I am part of a special team of Prison Chaplains. Occasionally, we are allocated to a specific individual if the powers that be deem it necessary. You happen to have been lucky, or unlucky, to have drawn me."

He paused to ascertain Legard's reaction to his deliberate falsehoods. It would not matter if Quentin Legard saw through him. The important point was that he held his tongue and trusted Luke sufficiently to allow Ray Quinn's plan time to work. Luke was a skilled and experienced interrogator and Legard's eyes gave him away. The outward scepticism could not hide the hope that Luke was gradually and inexorably instilling in him. The longer it went on, the more time they spent together, the deeper became Legard's reliance on Luke.

Luke sometimes, quite deliberately, missed the odd day. He watched the CCTV which showed Legard's cell on those occasions and each time it happened the more obvious Legard's discomfort became.

"That's enough for today," Luke declared suddenly.

"But we haven't finished the game," said Quentin, taken aback by the suddenness of Luke's statement.

"It will keep. We'll finish it tomorrow," said Luke.

He stood up, pushing his chair back with a scraping noise.

Legard thought quickly. "I'd like to pray, before you go."

"Not today." Luke turned away and took a stride towards the door.

Luke's actions were calculated. He was testing his charge and he was pleased by the result. He had manipulated their time together. At first, Quentin became reliant upon him, but that had now been transformed into real need.

On one occasion Luke missed two days. He swept into the cell the following day, looked the prisoner straight in the eyes and declared, "I think it's time we made progress. You need to unload." He took Legard by the arm and swept him out. He had no time to resist. He didn't realise that he was, quite literally, being swept off his feet. He had not considered the possibility that Luke could have such strength, and was amazed at this turn of events. He wasn't afraid; more surprised. Within a couple of moments, Legard was unceremoniously sat on a wooden pew in the Prison Chapel. Luke sat beside him, uncomfortably close.

"Don't talk. Just listen," commanded the priest. "We are here so that we cannot be overheard. You may not have realised it, but everything we've so far said in the cell has been recorded. I didn't know, but don't worry, I have the information. Nothing will come of it."

Luke was not telling the truth. He was moving the situation along so that his charge became even more needy. Now, to Legard, Luke was a man who had chosen to be on his side against the establishment. Luke gave him no time to consider the situation.

"We've come here because even the prison authorities would not dare to pry. When we began our time together I told you we would have to trust each other. I hope I have demonstrated that you may trust me. You need to understand something. I can get you out of here. I think you have believed that all along, but I'm telling you now that it's true. But you'll have to be patient. We must establish a pattern in order to divert attention and avoid suspicion. We'll come here every day from now on. We'll begin by playing chess in the cell as usual, so that our normal routine is maintained. Then we'll agree to pray here. People will get used to it and will accept it as our usual routine. It won't attract attention. After all, what could be more natural than a priest praying with a prisoner in the Chapel?"

Quentin Legard was confused. "I don't see how it will help me get out."

"Be patient," Luke whispered, as he lowered his head, as if beginning prayer. "I need you to tell me everything. All the things that you have done in your life that have led you here. If anybody hears, whether by accident or intention, it will sound as though you are making your confession; making your peace with God and seeking forgiveness."

"I've never told anybody such things!" Legard was appalled at the prospect of laying himself open. "How can I trust you? It's my life you are asking for."

"I had hoped I'd demonstrated that you can have absolute faith in me. However, ask yourself what choice you have. We'll begin tomorrow and by the end of it all there will be a way to get you out. It will take time, but, then, as I've pointed out before, that's something you have plenty of, isn't it?"

CONFESSION

-17-

"I'm really not happy about this," Legard said. "You're asking me to tell you about the things I've done and giving me nothing in return."

"You're not in a position to bargain," Luke said emphatically. "I've already told you, this is the only way. It's this or I'll walk away and you'll rot in jail. Also, you know that somebody will get to you. They always do. Nobody stays safe for ever in here. And it won't be pretty."

"I can look after myself," Legard said.

"No, you can't," replied Luke. "Not in here."

The silence could almost be touched, and it grew and grew. Neither man wanted to be the next to say anything. Finally, Luke lowered his head.

"Is there anything you have ever been afraid of?" he asked.

"No," Legard said.

"Are you afraid of what could happen to you in here?" Luke continued.

"No," Legard repeated.

"You should be," Luke said. "Are you afraid of me?"

"No," Legard continued his monosyllabic response.

"You should be," said Luke.

Quentin Legard thought for a moment and turned the tables.

"What scares you?" he asked.

"Nothing," replied Luke.

"So what's this all about?" asked Legard.

Luke let a moment pass and then said, "have you ever heard of a man called Ray Quinn?"

Legard thought before replying, and then lied. "No, I don't think so. Why do you ask?"

Luke moved a little closer and whispered in Quentin's ear. "Because he sent me here; to you, and he wants you out. You really don't want to disappoint him."

Legard was puzzled and it showed in his face. "He doesn't frighten me."

"Well he frightens me and I've served in some terrible places and seen horrible things," said Luke.

"Why does a complete stranger want to help me get out?" asked Legard.

"I'm sure he has his reasons. He hasn't told me what they are," replied Luke.

"If he's so scary, perhaps I'll just stay here and take my chances," Legard offered.

"Believe me, you don't want to do that. If you don't co-operate, then your life expectancy will be extremely short."

Quentin Legard weighed it all up and came to the conclusion that he was between a rock and a hard place. Whatever he decided the future did not look rosy. He shrugged his shoulders.

"Whatever," he said.

"Very sensible," Luke said. "Mr Quinn will be pleased to hear of your decision."

Luke then insisted they prayed. He knew it would have the desired effect of moving the situation on so that the process of confession could begin.

"Now, Quentin, let's begin with the rules. If you are to be helped you must hold nothing back. You must completely unburden yourself. You must leave nothing untold. Hide nothing. Also, be careful that you tell the truth. No exaggerations or embellishments. This is your only chance of salvation and then escape from here." Luke issued his instructions and waited.

"But, how will anybody know?" asked Legard.

"I'll know," answered Luke. "Everything you say will be checked, so it had better be right first time."

And so it was that Quentin Legard, multiple murderer, convicted criminal, began the story of his life.

He told of his childhood. He told Luke how his mother had become pregnant at the age of fourteen. She had been at boarding school and ran away before the school could send her away in disgrace. She gave birth to Quentin. She found herself alone in a squalid bedsit, and begged and scrounged to provide for her new born. She learned to survive at life's school of hard knocks. She accepted help from anywhere and anybody, and that had its dangers. She lost count of the unwanted advances from men who saw her as an easy opportunity. More than once that involved physically defending herself with a kitchen knife, leaving scars on whichever of their bodily parts were easiest to attack. Gradually she gained a reputation and the unwanted attentions diminished in number and ferocity.

When Quentin was less than a year old she met a man, several years her senior, who won her heart. Together they improved their situation, and eventually found a house on Exmoor. For Quentin this was his boyhood home and they grew as a family. No more children came along, so the young Legard was an only child. His surname was that of the man who had stood by his mother and the boy. He grew to love the man as his father. Indeed, he couldn't remember any details of his life before he came along.

He told Luke how his father had taught him to fish, swim and look after himself. He told how the family was happy but poor. His father eventually had to take a job that meant Quentin hardly spent any time with him. Despite this, to Quentin life was good. The only thing he felt odd was the fact that his mother would usher him out of the house at strange times during the day. He would be instructed not to return for an hour or two, and even then he must sit on the chair on the porch outside to wait for his mother to call him in. It was on one such occasion that his father had returned unexpectedly early from work and found the boy sitting waiting for his mother's call, just looking at the river as it flowed by. His father entered the house and Quentin's life changed for ever. He remembered a man with blood pouring from his nose sweeping past him and running away, limping badly as he screamed in terror. He remembered his mother's voice. He never forgot her begging and crying. He dare not enter the house. He just stood there, shaking as all went quiet. Sometime later his father had walked calmly through the front door and told Quentin to sit down.

The adult Quentin Legard now told Luke how his father had died, and could barely hold back his tears. He had watched as he deliberately walked calmly out into the fast flowing river that swept past their house, never to return. His father had told him that it was because his mother had been having an affair and he had disturbed her in their bed with the stranger when he returned home early from work. It transpired that it wasn't actually an affair. She had been selling herself for money to help make ends meet and his father had found out. He couldn't live with the shame. He explained to his son, Quentin, that he would have to be the man of the house and he must be brave. The young Quentin watched with disbelief, with tears streaming down his cheeks, as his father committed suicide.

The loss of his father was traumatic for Quentin. He never overcame the image of that calm walk to death. To the young boy it seemed that his father had shown incredible bravery, and he was determined not to let his father down. At that moment he vowed that he would not show physical fear and he bore life's vicissitudes with stoicism. He merely soaked them up and stored them for future use. He let them ferment and only reacted at a time of his choosing. For him, revenge was a dish best served cold, and he took control of its delivery.

The growing boy had known a father's love and now it had been snatched from him. He still loved his mother, but it was changed now. It had been tainted by what his father had told him. His understanding of love, whatever that was, had again been taken in another direction. His mother, ever practical, knew that she still had to provide for them. Her solution was to take in a lodger to help with the household income.

Needless to say there were tensions. Quentin had been told to call the lodger 'uncle.' This struck the boy as most strange. As far as he knew he hadn't got any uncles. He was bullied at school when classmates asked him which 'uncle' would be at home today. At first, he tried to answer their taunts but eventually gave up and didn't respond. He merely soaked it all up and made a mental note of the worst culprits. On one occasion he was chased by two older boys and his school jumper was torn. He knew his mother couldn't afford to replace it. Indeed she had scrimped and scraped so that his uniform was equal to everybody else's. He sat in class at the beginning of the afternoons lessons and cried. Not because he was afraid of the boys, but because he felt he had let his mother down by allowing it to happen. He knew she was always close to the end of her tether and any such setback might tip her over the edge. His vivid imagination saw her following his father and he cried. Loud, sobbing yelps. The rest of the class hid their smirks behind their hands, but their eyes gave away their contempt for him. He was providing more ammunition for them, but he couldn't help himself.

Luke listened quietly.

"So, what happened?" he asked.

"Nothing," replied Quentin. "My mother said absolutely nothing. She just stitched the jumper and put it out for me in the morning. It was remarkable. I was expecting all sorts of things, but nothing happened."

"What about your 'uncle'? Did he say anything?" asked Luke.

"No. He just watched as I told my mother and smiled to himself."

"That's odd," said Luke, "I would have expected him to say something."

"He didn't. Not then anyway. Later, just as I was about to go to bed, he took me outside and told me that I must never let my mother down like that again. I said she would not have been pleased if I had got involved in a fight with the boys at school. That would only have made it worse. He said I ought to make sure the bullies knew that I was not a pushover."

"Well, he was right about that, you know. If you let people push you around they will always come back for more," said Luke.

"I know," said Legard. "That's why I sorted it out myself a few weeks after."

"What did you do?" asked Luke.

"I waited at the bottom of a sloped path one lunchtime. I knew one of the boys who had torn my jumper would come running down the hill. I was round the corner of a building, so he didn't see me. There was a mirror opposite, so I could tell when he was coming. Just as he arrived at the corner at full speed, I swung my fist out as hard as I could. I felt the crunch as it hit his nose. He went down like a sack of potatoes, yelling at the top of his voice. I walked over to him and stamped on the hand that had torn my jumper. I heard crunching then as well."

"Effective," commented Luke.

"I thought so," said Legard.

"What did you feel? What did you feel like?" asked Luke.

"I didn't feel anything. My fist didn't hurt and my jumper had been mended. His jumper was covered in blood and I remember thinking it wouldn't be put right by stitching. I was satisfied by that. I knew he wouldn't pick on me anymore. I just walked away. Not my problem. It's funny, isn't it, how noses bleed so much?"

"Indeed they do. Why did you stamp on his hand?"

"Because it was the hand he had used to tear my jumper. I was very careful to get the right one," replied Legard.

"Do you remember anything else about the incident?" asked Luke.

"Yes," said Quentin. "I remember that it all happened slowly. I was in total control as if it was a slow motion film."

"How did you feel about that?" asked Luke, sitting up.

"Wonderful. Isn't that scary? Does that frighten you?" said Legard.

"Not at all," said Luke.

"Why not? It should. I could do it again," said Legard.

"You won't," said Luke. "You told me you're not a violent man."

"I may have lied," said Legard.

"That's possible, but I'm not worried," said Luke.

"Does anything frighten you? Or anybody?" asked Quentin.

"Just one," said Luke.

"Who?" asked Legard, curious now.

"We'll come to that in good time. Or, rather, you will. Then you'll know what fear really is." Luke said with finality.

"Perhaps," said Legard, unconvinced.

"Did anything happen after that?" asked Luke.

"If you mean, was I bullied again? Then no, I wasn't. The others left me alone from then on. The school did nothing either. They knew what had happened, of course, but they obviously decided it was best forgotten. No parent was going to complain. Just one of those things, I suppose. Boys will be boys."

"Do you want to pray, Quentin?" asked Luke.

"Not really," replied Legard. "Perhaps tomorrow. How much longer do we have to go on with this?"

"Until I think you're ready," replied Luke.

"Ready for what?" asked Legard, not prepared to leave it alone.

"Ready for what is to come," replied Luke.

"How will I know when that is?" asked Legard.

"You won't; I will," said Luke as he stood up and prepared to accompany his charge to his cell and return him to the loneliness of another long black night.

"Sweet dreams," Luke said and slammed the cell door shut.

QUENTIN'S NIGHTMARE
-18-

That night Quentin Legard had the first nightmare of his life. Most people have at least one before they become an adult, but Quentin had managed to avoid one until now. Perhaps it was his lonely incarceration, or the memories he had been encouraged to recall by Luke, but whatever the cause it was a devastating experience.   The following day he was able to recount it in vivid and accurate detail to Luke.

"I don't know what to think," he said to Luke, "but I want to tell you. Please don't interrupt me. Just listen until the end. I need to get this out."

He began.

"A few people, a very few people, are fortunate enough to finds a special kind of love. A love that's….well, just special. It goes far beyond anything there has ever been. Luke, I'm not talking about the kind of love you have with your mother or father. I'm talking about the kind of unquestioning love you can only have with a special woman. I've had plenty of women, Luke. I've been around."

Luke recognised that Quentin was being boastful. From what he already knew, Legard had cut a lonely figure thus far in his life. Luke also felt that boasting was not Quentin's usual style. It must be the dream. He did not interrupt. His role was to be the audience for the time being.

"Looking back, some of them were lovers," Quentin recommenced the story. "Some were just, you know, for the night. That sort of thing. Then I met her and I was helpless. She was special. Until then I didn't understand what love was all about. Special."

He tasted the word, nodding slowly.

Luke knew that Quentin was not an ignorant man. He wasn't particularly erudite, but he was smart. He had a certain cunning, which had been learned from an early age and honed in the burning furnace of real life. He had already owned up to his lack of high level education, which a lot of smart people never do.

"Special love. A love that rises above everything else," ventured Luke.

"Yes, that's it," said Legard, recognising the interruption but choosing to ignore it. "Have you ever loved like that?" he asked.

"Sort of," admitted Luke truthfully. "A long time ago."

He stopped there. He wasn't about to share his deepest personal life with Quentin Legard. He knew it was a recognised ploy of certain types of criminal mind to dig into the souls of their interlocutors, as a kind of quid pro quo. Who knew when such information might be used? It didn't matter, for at that moment Quentin Legard was far more interested talking about the woman who had become the centre of his universe.

"What's her name?" asked Luke, wanting to move the attention back to Quentin.

"Hannah," Legard answered, unable to mask soft awe in his voice. "The first time she told me her name I laughed. I don't know why, but I just did. It was as if it made me happy. As time went on, even the mention or thought of her name made me laugh."

Quentin nodded and smiled his trademark smile. "You've got a nice smile Luke, but you're not a patch on her!" he joked.

Luke laughed and repressed a yawn at the same time. The day was passing with unseemly haste and Luke wanted, actually needed, his charge to get on with it. He couldn't press, however. He knew that Legard relating his nightmare in detail was a significant event. It would, he hoped, be the key that would unlock the next stage of the plan.

"There's a gap in the dream now," said Legard. All I can remember is that I had trouble with her father." He scoffed. "The bastard. It's not a nice tale, Luke."

"Tell me," Luke said softly, moving forward to show interest.

Quentin concentrated and crossed his strong hands, interlocking his fingers. Luke noticed for the first time just how strong he must be.

"For some reason I was in an emergency department in a hospital, I don't know where or why, but the nurse was Hannah. She jabbed me with tetanus and stitched me up. I didn't feel a thing. I was numb. All I could see was that wonderful woman. She told me how to wash the wound and change the dressing. Do you believe in fate?" he asked.

"Well, that's a huge debate, especially for a priest like me," answered Luke, not wishing to slow the story.

"Does that mean yes or no?" Legard insisted, frowning.

"Well, if you insist, I do, in a way, with certain reservations," Luke said.

"Well, you better get your act together, because there is such a thing." Love had tamed his irascibility and he was grinning. "Hannah and me, we were fated to be together. We were fated to meet there and then. Oh, Luke, she was fantastic. I mean, there I was with a four inch gash in my arm, twenty stitches; I could have bled to death. Yet nothing mattered. All I could think about was that I was facing the most beautiful woman in the world. Her hair was blonde. Natural, not from a bottle. Her body; Oh my god, her body! Sorry, No offence intended."

"None taken," Luke answered.

"I asked her out, there and then," Legard continued. "On the spot. In the emergency room. How many times must that happen to a pretty nurse? She was probably trying to think of a way to get rid of yet another idiot, but something gave her away. I can read people. Words and looks can be two different things and I was getting the message. She said that there was a rule never to date patients. I wasn't going to leave it there, so I returned next day with a dozen red roses. She pretended that she didn't remember me and asked what room they were for. I told her they were for her, if she had room in her heart for me. Corny line, but it worked."

Luke settled back to listen. Quentin was in full flow.

"The first date was magic. We had dinner at a fancy restaurant. Cost me an arm and a leg. I was embarrassed because I hadn't worn a jacket or tie. They made me wear one of theirs. I swear they keep the most awful ones just for the purpose. It didn't fit very well and I knew I looked stupid, but neither of us cared. Heavens, she was the most beautiful thing

I'd ever seen. We were there for three or four hours. She was quite shy and didn't say much. Like an idiot I just talked and talked and talked. I realised I wasn't making any sense because I was looking at her and not paying any attention to what I was saying. We drank a whole bottle of wine. It cost me a lot of money, but I didn't even care about that. I didn't care about anything, Luke. I even told her about everything I'd done. Especially the things I'm not proud of."

Luke supressed a smile. Quentin had taken a huge step.

"Have you ever confessed everything?" asked Legard. "I'll know if you lie."

Luke was stumped. He also knew Quentin would recognise a lie, so decided to be honest.

"Actually, I have. But that's for another time. I'll tell all later. Please continue," Luke hoped he had diverted him.

"To continue, then," Legard said, settling in for the long haul. "The next thing I knew was that the sky lit up outside. Fireworks everywhere. Even I thought it was a sign from the man upstairs. We watched from the window."

His eyes gleamed as he went on. "I took her home and we stood on the steps of her parents' house. She was still living with them. We talked for a while longer and then she said she had to get to bed. I think she deliberately put the word 'bed' in there, just to give me a message. She could have said she had 'to be going' or just 'goodnight' but she didn't. I can assure you it was not my imagination working overtime."

He paused to relive the moment.

"The next day," he continued eventually," I kept getting distracted. I couldn't concentrate on anything. I used the internet and found some information about her family. It turns out they are filthy rich. I mean, loaded. Rolling in it. Houses and holiday homes all over the place. Then I read about her father. An actual tycoon, but not in a nice way, if you know what I mean. He owns a company and a lot more besides. He is tough. A big man, not fat, just tough. His eyes look you over like he couldn't care less about you. He knows he could crush you like an insect. He sizes you up. He knows you. He gets inside your head. He knows what you are thinking about his daughter. What every father knows, because they were young once. We caught sight of each other when I dropped her off, and I knew, I just knew, that we were heading for trouble. I didn't really think too much about it then, but deep inside the thought was there."

Luke spotted that Legard had not mentioned her mother. This dream was lacking that significant detail. He had blocked the woman out. It reflected his real life.

"What about her mother?" Luke asked.

"Her mother? She doesn't come into it at all." Quentin blocked this line of discussion with finality. "It was her father who was getting at me. I think it was because Hannah was an only child."

Quentin lapsed into silence and showed no sign of recommencing the tale of his dream

"Please continue," Luke said, wanting to move things along, but at the same time be polite in order to get the best from Legard.

"Don't rush me!" shouted Legard suddenly. Again, he seemed to need silence for a while. Eventually he drew a deep breath and said, "Our second date went even better than the first. We saw a film. I can't remember what it was. Then I drove her home...." His voice trailed away. Then he said, "I asked her out for a few days after that but she couldn't make it. The same thing happened for some time and I got annoyed. You don't want to see me angry."

Luke looked up into his face and decided not to make any comment. He would continue in his own time, preferably after any anger had passed.

Legard began again, "I wondered whether she was trying to dump me; you know, get rid of me. After a while she explained it. She said she was working two shifts whenever she could, which I thought was strange. I mean, her father is absolutely loaded and his daughter, his beloved only child, is working double shifts. I realized it couldn't have been for the money, unless her father was not supporting her at all. Perhaps he was one of those parents who believed a child needs to grow up and stand on her own two feet; learn the meaning of money and what it takes to get it. In the end I worked it out. She was just like me. Independent. She dropped out of college to work at the hospital because she was saving her own money to travel. She didn't want to owe her parents anything."

"Brave young woman," commented Luke.

"Oh she was more than that," said Quentin. "Oh, so much more. It made me more in love with her than ever. I mean, I had found a woman who actually had a mind of her own, and could connect with me. I love that."

"Do you now?" Luke asked, but the irony was lost on Quentin Legard.

"In the back of my mind I was thinking about all the places I'd like to go with her. On our first date she had told me that she loved poetry, so I wrote her poems about travelling. It's funny, but I'd never written anything like that in my life before and there I was with poetry just pouring out of me. Hundreds of the damn things. They probably weren't much good, but I didn't care and Hannah seemed to love each and every one." Legard was in full flow now and Luke was afraid that he would begin spouting poetry there and then, which would slow proceedings down somewhat.

Luke shifted his position to indicate his impatience. It was the next best thing to openly looking at his watch.

Legard took the not so subtle hint. "Well, I suddenly realised we were in love. I knew this was dangerous ground for me, what with my history, but I couldn't help it. I now understood why there are so many soppy songs about love. My heart was singing itself. I understood; I got it; I really had it. Ours was a special love and I could think about nothing else. Just two weeks and we were completely in love. I couldn't wait, I was ready to propose. I borrowed some money and bought a diamond ring."

Quentin caught the look on Luke's face, and scowled in return.

"I asked her out to dinner on Friday. I was going to give the ring to a waiter and ask him to put it on a plate and bring it when we ordered dessert." Legard gazed into the distance. "I got to her house early. There were cars all over the place. Hannah came to the door and stepped outside. She looked nervous and I knew something was wrong. My stomach knotted. She said her mother was having a party and there was a problem. She said she had to stay and help and that she'd see me in a day or two."

Luke saw the pain in Legard's eyes. He was shocked. He hadn't thought of him as being capable of such deep emotion. He thought it had been sucked from him by then. He then saw that Legard's eyes had turned as dead as rocks.

"But I knew there was more to it. Much more. There had to be," whispered Legard.

"Hannah's father, you mean?" said Luke quietly.

Legard did not explain. He merely returned to his story. "That was one of the worst nights of my life."

Knowing Legard's history Luke doubted that somehow, but opted not to argue.

"I mean," Legard was speaking again, "I'd borrowed a lot of money, got there early, planned the whole thing and I couldn't even get five minutes with her. What would you do?"

Luke was about to answer when Legard went on, "I drove around all night. Woke up at dawn, in my car, by the railway station. When I got home there wasn't even a message from her. I can't tell you how I felt. I have no words to describe it."

Luke felt Quentin's inability to put words to his emotion was worrying and clenched his fists in anticipation.

I phoned her at the hospital that morning and she said she was sorry about the party, so I asked her out that night. She said she really shouldn't, she was so tired because the party had gone on into the early hours. She said she could make tomorrow."

A gleam returned to Legard's eyes. Luke thought the gleam reflected a pleasant memory of their next date, but he was wrong. Legard's voice grew bitter.

"I learned a lesson that night, Luke," said Legard.

"What lesson would that be?" queried Luke.

"It's a mistake to underestimate your enemy. Listen to me. Don't ever do it." He looked directly into Luke's eyes, which the priest had to admit later shook him.

"Anyway," Legard continued, I went over the next night to pick her up. I was going to drive out into the country. I know a nice peaceful place where we wouldn't be disturbed. I'll show it to you when I get out."

Luke caught the sinister undertone and decided that was one offer he would not be accepting.

"I was going to propose. I had prepared a speech. I knew it off by heart. I'd go down on one knee; you know, the whole nine yards. I drove up to her house and she waved to me. God, she was so beautiful. I just wanted to hold her; take her in my arms and hold her forever and not let go."

Quentin savoured the memory for a while.

"But something was wrong. She was distant. You must have had that happen to you. The moment when you know there's a problem and your stomach flutters. She stepped away from me and kept glancing into the house. Her face was pale and her hair was tied back. It looked severe and I didn't like it. I'd already told her I liked it when she let it down." Quentin seemed lost.

Luke noted that Legard became stern and steely when anybody did anything he didn't like or went against his wishes. It was not a nice trait; in fact Luke saw it as threatening and less assured men would have been afraid at that moment.

"I thought the hair being tied back was a kind of signal. Perhaps she needed help," said Legard. "I asked her what the problem was and she began to cry. That floored me, I can tell you. I can't cope with a woman crying. It's something to do with my mother I suppose."

He took a few moments to compose himself before he could carry on. "She said I should go and not come back. She wouldn't go into details however hard I tried. She just kept looking round and I realised there was somebody inside the door, listening. She was obviously scared to death. She kept begging me to leave, not to call her or come back again. I caught on. I'm not stupid, you know."

He stopped his narrative, seeking Luke's agreement.

None was forthcoming, so he continued, "I realised she was saying those things over and over for the benefit of whoever was behind the door, spying on us. I said, loudly, that if that's the way she wanted it, then fine. But at the same time, I pulled her close into me and whispered for her not to worry. I would sort it out. She hugged me and then let me go. I walked away. It was not a pleasant walk at all."

Luke noted the understatement. "He's learning," he thought.

"That night was one of the longest of my life. I waited for as long as I could cope with it and phoned her. I just had to hear her voice. I had to. I needed her as much as food or water or oxygen. Nobody picked up the phone and I didn't leave a message. I didn't sleep at all that weekend; not one single hour. I knew what had happened. I knew exactly. It wasn't difficult."

Luke realised the story of the dream was taking a long time, but knew it was significant. It was a turning point, so he had to allow it to continue for as long as it took. There were so many things happening on all sorts of levels that a psychiatrist would have had a field day. Perhaps he would let somebody have the recording he was making when it was all over. He was jolted back to the present when Legard started again.

"I had to talk to her. I went to the hospital at six on Monday morning and just waited for her to arrive. She saw me. She looked afraid, but came over to me. She kept looking round as if somebody was following her. I didn't waste time. I told her I knew it was her father who was the problem. It wasn't a question. It was a statement because I knew. She sniffled and nodded and told me that she'd been forbidden from seeing me. That hurt me. I mean, the man hadn't even met me! He didn't know me!"

"Just as well," Luke thought.

"I thought it was so old-fashioned. Who did he think he was? The bastard! Hannah was crying by now. She begged me to leave, and tried to pull away."

Quentin Legard seemed to be struggling to cope with his emotions. Luke watched him carefully, like a predator watches dangerous prey, aware that the tables could be turned.

"You see, Luke," Legard continued, "love means nothing to men like her father. It's all about image, money, society, social standing; that's what counts to bastards like that. I couldn't take it anymore. I put my arms around her and said we should just get out. There. Then. No messing. I was desperate. I wanted us to be together and to hell with anything else. Have you ever felt like that about anybody?" he asked.

"No," Luke lied. He wasn't about to share such intimacy with a man like Quentin Legard. It was too dangerous. You never knew what could happen in the future.

"I don't believe you," said Legard. "Anyway; no matter. Hannah just told me to leave and was looking around all the time. Then I saw what she was looking for. Her father had sent one of his thugs to spy on her. He had spotted us and was running our way. I didn't move. I knew I could deal with him. He was nothing to me; a fly to be crushed. If he touched her I was going to break his neck. Hannah begged me to run, but I put my arms round her and said we should get away together. One part of me wanted to run with her, but another part wanted the man to challenge me. It would have been his last act. Hannah said he was armed, but I said I didn't care, even though a gun changed the situation. She said she didn't want me to get hurt and the thug wouldn't hurt her if I went. Then I asked her if she loved me. I had to know. I had to be sure, because it would tell me what to do next. She looked at me with tears in the corners of her eyes and promised that she did. That was enough for me. I knew we could sort it out. Not there. Not then. But we would make it; together."

Quentin Legard had to pause to catch his breath and to turn away so that Luke could not see his tears.

"Can we leave it for now?" he asked. "I need time to think. I'm going to tell you the rest of the dream. It becomes more of a nightmare, if it hasn't already been just that."

Luke wondered what Legard was playing at. He preferred to continue, but his charge was obviously in need of rest.

"Are you going to be alright?" he asked.

"Don't worry," answered Legard. I'll finish it tomorrow. You might be surprised."

"So might you," said Luke, laconically. "Do you want to pray before I go?"

"No thanks," replied Legard. "Perhaps when I've got it all off my chest. That may be a good time."

"Oh, yes," thought Luke, "you'll be in need of prayer then. Good night."

"Is he ready?" asked the voice.

"Nearly," replied Luke. "Tomorrow will see it done."

"Excellent. Thank you. Call me tomorrow?"

"Of course," promised Luke.

QUENTIN'S NIGHTMARE CONTINUED
-19-

"I threw myself back into my normal routine. I didn't want anybody to be suspicious. I kept writing her poetry, sending her letters. I put fake return addresses so her father wouldn't know it was me. Stupid, I know. He must have realised. Occasionally, I'd see her in person. Once we even had coffee together. She was happy to see me, but was nervous because her father had put minders on her and they followed her everywhere. One of them saw us and I had to get out through the window at the back of the café. After that I noticed black cars with darkened windows began to follow me down the street, keeping an eye on me."

Quentin had restarted the tale of his dream as promised the following morning. He seemed more determined than the day before to get it over with. It was as if he was approaching a conclusion that had significance for him.

"Then one of the men who'd been following me walked up to me, bold as brass, and said I would get ten thousand to go away and never come back. I just laughed. I wasn't going to throw away the special love I had found before I'd even had time to savour it. To share it. I snapped. I grabbed him and shoved him against a wall. He couldn't do anything. He was pathetic. Not even a challenge. I told him to go back to her father and tell him to shove his money. I told him to say that if he didn't leave us alone he would bring something on himself that he couldn't imagine; something the like of which he'd never experienced in his life. I gave him a good kicking and sent him on his way."

Legard laughed loudly at the memory. "I don't think her father took the hint, but that man didn't come back. That's the trouble with fathers, I think. Fathers are jealous; they hate their daughter's boyfriends because they remember what they themselves were like when they were single and young. They fear being replaced. It's like a slap in the face. Their daughters are transferring their love to another male. What very few of them realise is that it's a different kind of love. It's not rejection, nor is it replacement."

Luke was impressed by Legard's understanding.

"The trouble was her father didn't understand at all. Or, more likely, he chose not to for some reason," Legard began again. "He ignored my message. I went to the hospital one day and was told that Hannah had left. Her father had phoned and told them she was leaving. She had cleaned out her locker. I called the house, but the number had changed and was now unobtainable. I have to hand it to him, the man was determined. He didn't stop there. He started to have notes left in my letterbox. Threats. He knew I wouldn't go to the police because I appreciated how much money he had and money is power."

Legard's demeanour changed and his body tensed.

"That was when I decided to play by my own rules."

He leaned forward and touched Luke's hand. The priest felt the energy and insistent pulse on his skin.

"Hannah is so fragile, you know. So delicate. I had to do something. She had no defence against her father. I went to the police. Me! Can you imagine? Me, going to the police!" Legard paused, still amazed by his own action. "I wanted them to go to the house and see if she was alright. But it was also a message to her father that I wasn't a man to be messed with. It was a mistake, Luke, I made a mistake."

"Explain," ordered Luke.

"He was one step ahead of me. I was pushed into a corner by a large policeman and told that if I didn't stay away from Hannah and her family a restraining order would be taken out, and I'd end up in a cell. Then he smiled and said that all sorts of accidents happened to prisoners. Jail could be a dangerous place, he said. You know, he even had the cheek to smile as he said it."

"Money is power," Luke echoed Quentin's earlier remark. Then he noticed that Legard's face had changed. It had become serene.

"Hannah gave me a signal. I was hiding in the bushes near her house, watching with binoculars. I just wanted to see her. I wanted to make sure she was alright. She must have seen me because she raised the blind. The light was behind her and it made her hair glow. She had an aura, literally and figuratively. I could see the outline of her body beneath her nightgown. She was an angel and she was showing me that she missed me."

Legard stopped his tale and gazed into the distance. Luke let him take his own time.

"I spent the next week planning. I thought we could run away. I was going to rescue her. I was going to challenge her old man. I found out he was away on business for a few days and I knew our chance had come. I went to the house. It was pouring with rain, which helped. I broke in through the kitchen window, went up to her room and just guided her out. It was that easy. We didn't have any cases or bags. We just had each other. We were free! And happy. No, happy doesn't describe it. We were ecstatic."

Luke eased himself back and prepared for Legard to continue.

"I drove for miles and miles. I kept to whatever limit each road carried, to avoid attracting unwanted attention."

"Sensible," commented Luke.

"I thought so," said Quentin, "I thought it would be difficult for him to follow us because he would have to explain his treatment of his daughter. But I'd made a mistake."

"You underestimated the opposition," offered Luke.

"Exactly," said Legard. "How did you know?"

"Because money is power," said Luke.

"Yes, you're right," said Legard. "He had friends everywhere. We spotted them when we stopped for something to eat. One of them came in and asked about a couple who were on the run. They made it sound like Bonnie and Clyde. I said we needed to get off the road and hide for a while. We ended up at the end of a narrow track in a forest. We spent the whole day there, laying in the grass together, her head resting on my chest. We slept and talked. It was so peaceful."

Luke respected the silence. Time was pressing but he could afford to be generous.

"We didn't," said Legard. "We wanted to, we could have, but both of us said nothing and we just knew it would be better if we waited. Then things got difficult. A car passed us and slammed on its brakes. It turned round and came straight towards us. I recognized it immediately. It was her father's men. I've never driven as fast as I did then. Eventually we had more and more cars after us and I knew we would have to split up. I found an abandoned place and dropped her off there."

Quentin looked forlorn. Luke almost felt compassion for him.

"We held each other for a while before we parted and I made sure she had gone in before I left. If her father got his hands on her I knew he'd send her away. Our plan was that she'd hide there for a while and I would lead them away as far as possible. Then I'd wait for him and confront him. Believe me, I can do certain things."

"I don't doubt it," said Luke.

"I wasn't planning to kill him. I just wanted to show him he couldn't go on like this. Hannah begged me not to. She knew how dangerous he could be. I didn't care, though. I knew he'd never leave us alone if I didn't do something."

Legard rose and walked around the prison chapel, muttering to himself. Luke watched him carefully and made sure his back was never turned.

"After a while I had to leave her, so I drove away. I'll never forget her face in the mirror getting smaller and smaller. I was busy watching her as I drove and it was then that I had to stop. My car was being surrounded by other vehicles and I had nowhere to go. A man got out of one of them and stormed towards my car. I recognised him immediately. It was her father. I don't know how he managed to be there, but there he most certainly was. He had quite a few men behind him, so I knew I was in trouble, but I wasn't afraid." Legard paused.

Luke wondered why Legard kept stressing the point that he was not afraid. It was as if it was important to him that nobody saw fear in him. Perhaps he thought of it as a sign of weakness. It surely couldn't be true that he had not been afraid of anything in his life so far. That would be incredible. Luke knew he would have to face it before long and almost felt sorry for him. Quentin had yet to learn that it could be a useful tool and Luke doubted he ever would.

Legard began again. "He didn't do anything, which surprised me. I was ready and he disappointed me. All that happened was that he begged me to tell him where his daughter was. I mean, we know money is power but I had beaten him with a greater power; the power of love. I actually found it disappointing when he just turned on his heels and walked back to his car."

Silence fell between Luke and Legard, but Luke wasn't in the mood to let it develop and linger. He wanted to drive today's session to the conclusion that had been planned. It was late at night, but neither man showed signs of fatigue. Legard had been pacing up and down, but stopped suddenly and looked up to the ceiling. Outside it was pitch black and the rain had stopped its beating on the roof. The wind, however, howled as if in pain as it drove dark clouds across the sky.

Luke delved beneath his priestly robes until his fingers wrapped themselves around his mobile phone. He found the button he was searching for and pressed. There was no noise; no tell-tale beep. Luke had managed to smuggle the object into the session because the prison guards had grown tired of searching the priest day after day. They had grown to trust him. The daily grinding routine of their lives had dulled their edge. It was important that it remained undiscovered because there could later be no blame attached to the prison staff. They would later confirm that they had searched the priest as was their usual practice and nothing had been found.

There was a solid rap on the chapel door, which swung open, but there was nobody standing in the doorway. It was as if the door had somehow been opened by an unseen force. A distant clock started to strike twelve. Midnight. The witching hour. In the USA it's the traditional time when prisoners are taken from their cell on Death Row for a short walk to meet their maker.

"It's time, Quentin," said Luke.

The priest stretched out his right arm and, palm open, indicated to Legard that he should precede him through the open door. Legard hesitated, unsure and wondering. There was nobody in the narrow corridor. Quentin was suddenly conscious of the fact that it was not the door through which they had entered the chapel and the corridor was not the one they normally used.

"Please, go on, we haven't got much time," encouraged Luke.

"What's happening? Where are we going?" Legard asked, his voice betraying a quivering uncertainty.

"It's alright, Quentin. "Don't worry," said Luke as he produced a slim document from beneath his robes. "This is for you." He gave the black leather covered folder to Legard. "There's no time to read it now. Save it for later. It makes good reading, I think. Now, please, let's hurry."

The two men moved swiftly along, one after the other, aiming for the doorway at the end of the corridor. When they arrived in front of the door, Legard stepped aside, flattening himself against the wall. He wanted Luke to go through the door first. He had just lost his faith in the priest.

"Don't worry," said Luke, as he opened the door and walked through without any hesitation at all. By the time

Quentin Legard had followed him and caught up, Luke had a Bible in his hand and had started to read aloud in sombre tones that echoed and took an eternity to fade.

LUKE THE TEACHER
-20-

"Wake up, Quentin."

Frank slapped Legard hard across both cheeks and continued until they were livid pink. Gradually his prisoner stirred and moaned. His head jerked from side to side with each slap and a thin line of spittle dribbled from the right corner of his mouth. Frank had discarded his robes and was now dressed from head to toe in black. He stood leaning over Quentin Legard, who was strapped firmly onto a wooden palette. They were in a disused warehouse located on the outskirts of a retail park, whose most prosperous days were long gone. There was no chance of noise carrying outside the building and even less chance of their being disturbed by any unwanted intrusion.

"Listen to me," Frank ordered. "Listen very carefully."

Legard tried, unsuccessfully to move.

"Don't waste your energy, Quentin. You're going to need it."

Legard knew the words were true. He was in the hands of a professional and all he could do was to be passive, allow his head to clear and wait. But he had questions.

"My nightmare; I was telling you my nightmare," he said.

"I know," said Frank. "Look at me. Do you recognise me?"

"You're....you're the priest."

"Yes," said Frank, "but you may still call me Luke. I am still your teacher and you still have lessons to learn."

"Where am I?" asked Legard.

"That doesn't matter at the moment," replied Frank. "Try to relax. You're not in danger. We have plenty of time now. You are not in prison now, so you could say you are in a better place."

"I don't understand," said Legard.

"All in good time. Be patient. As I said, we have plenty of time." Frank said.

Quentin Legard stopped questioning Luke. He sighed and cast his gaze up at the ceiling. Awake now, he was searching for clues. He knew he was physically constrained, but he reasoned that did not mean he couldn't use his wits. He tried to concentrate upon details. He tried to pick up things that might be useful later. It had worked for him before and he hoped it would save him now. The fightback was beginning.

Frank saw it all. "Don't bother. Just settle down and let it happen. The sooner we get on, the sooner your troubles will be over."

The prisoner closed his eyes in acquiescence.

"Now, before we left the prison you were telling me about your nightmare. Do you remember?" asked Frank.

"Yes." Legard had decided to say as little as possible.

"Well, the nightmare is over. It ended with you thinking you were going to meet your maker. The dream was real enough, Quentin, and it told me a great deal about you."

"Really? What was that?" Legard queried.

"That you are not easily frightened; that your life has been one long nightmare; that you are in a dark place; that you scare people; that you've been a very naughty boy; that you need to make amends." Frank stopped. "I could go on, but that's enough to be going on with."

Legard decided not to say anything. Confronted by the uncomfortable truth, silence was the safest thing. But he still had questions.

"How did you manage to get me out?" he asked.

"That doesn't matter. It is irrelevant," answered Frank. "From now on, we'll only be dealing in necessities."

Again Legard lapsed into silence.

"I think we should make a start, don't you?" whispered Frank, close to his captive's right ear.

He moved away from his prone prisoner. Legard couldn't see what he was doing, but his imagination was working overtime and he did not like what it was saying to him. Frank was not actually doing anything except moving about making a noise. He was deliberately making his captive wait and think. Ray Quinn had taught him that the anticipation of pain was worse than the actuality. Eventually he returned to Legard.

"Right, let's sit you up and make you comfortable."

Legard was hoisted, still strapped immovably to the wooden palette, so that he was upright. He faced a large screen.

"Now Quentin, you're going to the cinema. I'm afraid I haven't got any popcorn. Sorry about that."

Connections 5 I NEED A WORD PAUL STUART

Legard was silent as he took in the white screen facing him.

Frank continued, "it seems you've been less than honest with me, and that's most unfortunate. You promised me you would confess everything. I know you omitted certain events and I'm going to show you what they are. When we've finished, please let me know if I've missed anything out. I don't think I have, but you never know. Oh, I almost forgot to mention, you may recognise yourself as one of the characters in each of the films. The names might be different and details of the lives of the actual people do not match your own, but I'm sure you'll work it out. We are more interested in examining your character and what makes you tick. It's quite interesting work. It's really a case of 'if the cap fits......"

Frank did not need to dim the lights. The place was dark enough already because it had no windows. Legard had no choice but to watch. He already knew what he was about to see and was intrigued to find out if Luke had been thorough in his research. He was about to confronted by some uncomfortable viewing. The screen flickered and the first film began.

FILM ONE: THE FIRST LESSON
-21-

The film was not a film in the usual sense. It was more of a written story and Legard had to read it rather than passively watch. It made him more involved and, as a result, more uncomfortable. He was puzzled.

"Why not just give me the story and let me read it, like a book?" He asked.

"I want to watch you as you look at the screen. I want to see your eyes as you experience it. I look forward to a worthwhile learning experience. The folder I gave you earlier is the document itself, but you are going to watch it on the screen. You can keep the paperwork when this is over. Consider it a memento. A gift, from your teacher."

Frank's explanation was over, but what he had not told his captive was that it wasn't just Frank who would be watching. Another pair of eyes were taking a keen interest.

He knew he didn't really stand a chance with her, of course. She was, all too obviously, out of his league. Nevertheless, Richard Porter, forty-four in age and waistband, couldn't help being seduced by the sight of the resident in number 4 when she had moved into his apartment building six months ago. After all, a man can dream can't he? Richard certainly dreamed. With focused hopes but diffuse energy, Porter had moved to London two years ago, but had failed miserably to find employment. He had fired off seemingly hundreds of applications and CV's, but none had been successful. He didn't appear to fit anybody's concept of an ideal employee, so he set up on his own, labelling himself as a Contract Consultant. He advertised widely at first, but as his reputation grew that need was reduced. He settled into a pleasant enough routine and was reasonably content.

The fly in the ointment was his love life; or, to be more accurate, the lack of it. He was single. He'd had some experiences but had always found it hard to connect with a woman on a serious level. None of the women he went out with, mostly blind dates, knew much at all about anything he was interested in. Some of them only wanted to rant about their ex-husbands or other partners. His dates tended to dress themselves with unglamorous clothes and were generally solid in stature.

He had come across a few attractive women. Lisa Richards, for example, had been one. He'd met her when he fulfilled a contract for her and pursued her to The White Horse Inn at Exford. He had high hopes of that relationship, but it eventually petered out. He never found out the real reason, but he knew he always found himself longing for greener pastures in the women department. He couldn't help it. It was just the way he was. He suspected that Lisa had rumbled him and fled for the hills.

Now he was living in a place that in reality was a massive inventory of the most gorgeous women on earth. They were also not just pretty. They had substance to go with looks. He thought he had died and gone heaven, which, when he considered his life, was extremely unlikely. He'd sit in coffee shops listening to them and was enthralled. The bonus was that they wore tight fitting clothes and seemed to enjoy flaunting themselves. He often thought that they wouldn't be so careless if they only knew what he was thinking.

Richard Porter had virtually given up on romance. The appearance of the new resident of number 4 changed that. Her name was Tessa Goldberg. He had found that out from one of the maintenance men the morning after she had moved in. She was gorgeous, with long hair which was as black as raven's wings. She was tall, slim and fit. She ran every day and sometimes he'd spot her standing in the cool, foggy air, practicing some kind of martial art and stretching her lithe body into impossible positions. There were several people in his apartment block who took exercise every day and he had names for each of them. Puffing Billly was always found walking his dog, almost lost in a cloud of cigarette smoke; the Tone Deaf Singer announced his morning run by singing at the top of his voice with his earphones firmly in place. His eyes apparently noticed nothing in his path and was totally oblivious to anyone or anything around him. He was in the process of giving many others nicknames, but the arrival of the vision that was Tessa stopped him in his tracks.

He was also drawn by the fact that she had a great joy of life. She apparently travelled a good deal and, according to what he'd been told, she had a home elsewhere and often spent weekends there. Richard Porter imagined them spending time together there, undisturbed by life's stresses and strains. She had a scooter, much like those driven by the Mods in the sixties, and she also drove a battered old sports car, which she drove at reckless speeds.

He fell into the practice of observing her on a daily basis. She left her apartment each morning carrying a small portfolio type case and he wondered what it contained. He convinced himself that she would agree to go out with him and that it may develop into something serious. His relationships normally followed the same pattern, and it usually ended in tears. He always started out with high hopes and they were never satisfied. He thought of himself as reasonably attractive as a man. Perhaps he was a touch portly, but women like a man of substance don't they? He didn't smoke and only drank in moderation. He didn't have money worries and always paid his way. All things considered, he was a good proposition, he thought.

The problem was that doubts always swarmed like bees. He was actually shy. How could he meet her? Certainly, simply walking up to her and introducing himself was too obvious. You only get one chance at a first impression and that was not it. For months he worshipped her from afar; struggling to come up with some way to break the ice without making a fool of himself.

Then, one fine day, he got a break. He was standing by his window, as had become his habit at around seven each evening, when he noticed movement from the bushes across the pavement from Tessa's bedroom. There was a moment's pause and then it happened again. This time he saw a faint flash of light, like a reflection from glass. He hurried across his room and switched out the light. He also pulled the blinds down. He could still see out by kneeling down and peering under the blind. He was shocked to spot a man crouching in the bushes. He appeared to be staring into Tessa's window. He was dressed in the uniform of the staff maintenance men. Porter rose from his knees and slipped into his bedroom, from where he thought he would get a better view. He was certain. There was absolutely no doubt the skinny man was watching and stalking her. He had binoculars, for heaven's sake.

Porter's initial reaction, his gut instinct, was to call the police and he got as far as holding the phone. Something stopped him, however. The thought struck him that there may be a way he could use the situation to his advantage. He put the phone down. Tessa's curtains closed, so he moved his attention to concentrate on the stalker. He saw the pervert's shoulders slump in clear disappointment, as if he was waiting for her to undress for a shower or something. The stalker did not move, preferring to remain in position, waiting for an opportunity to begin his watching again. He stayed in position, waiting for a chance to resume his spying. But then Tessa's door opened and she stepped outside. She was wearing her pink top and tight floral trousers. Her blue leather bag was over her shoulder and sunglasses rode high on her head, stuck into her hair, which was loose tonight. The man crouched down into the bushes, out of sight.

Tessa locked her door and walked down the path towards the car park. Where was the maintenance man? But just as Porter snatched up the phone and started to tap away he saw the stalker rise. He hadn't been about to pounce; he'd only been gathering up his tools. Carrying them, he turned away from Tessa and walked in the opposite direction, towards the back of the building.

Tessa disappeared into the car park and, moments later, the rattle of her MG engine and the whine of gears filled the night as she sped away in the little green car.

That evening Porter stayed close to home, ordering in a pizza and keeping a close eye on any movement outside. He was ready to take special note of anything out of the ordinary; anything that was not part of the normal routine of the area and its inhabitants. Hours passed without any sign of Tessa or her stalker, and there was nothing exceptional to note either. He nearly fell asleep, but he made some coffee, drank it down black and hot, and forced himself to stay awake so he could continue his vigil. He reflected, with a shiver of excitement, that this was just like the Hitchcock thriller Rear Window; where James Stewart, housebound in a wheelchair, spent his time peering through his neighbours' windows. It was one of Porter's favourite films and he wondered whether Tessa had ever seen it. He had a feeling she had.

At nine pm, still seeing no sign of Tessa or the skinny stalker, Porter decided to be proactive. He went downstairs and around the back of the building, where he found the manager.

"Who's the young maintenance man? The blond haired one?" he asked. Although he wanted the information he did not bother to be overly polite and the manager was not impressed.

"Blond?" the heavyset man asked, pulling a strand of greasy hair from his forehead. He smelled of beer.

"Yes; the short one." Porter said curtly.

"You said blond?" responded the manager.

"Right, the one with the blond hair," Porter said, frowning in frustration. He felt the manager was being deliberately obstructive and unhelpful. "You understand who I mean?"

The manager did not appear to be of foreign origin, so there should have been no language barrier. Perhaps he was just stupid.

"I thought, you called somebody 'the blonde', that meant a girl." The manager smiled at how obtuse he had managed to be.

"Well, I'm asking about a blond haired man. He's short. He was trimming hedges and raking today. You know who I mean?" asked Porter, the impatience clearly showing now.

"Yes, I know him," came the reply.

"What's his name?" asked Porter.

"I don't know. I didn't hire him. He just turned up to work." He gave Porter a hard stare, trying to indicate how annoyed he was becoming at the impertinent questioning.

"What's his story," persisted Porter, ignoring the stare.

"Story? I don't know. He sweeps up, he rakes and he cuts the grass. That's the story as far as I know. Why?"

"So don't you know anything about him?" Porter was becoming increasingly agitated now.

"Why?" The manager was now defensive, suspicious of the reasoning behind the incessant questioning.

"Just curious," said Porter.

Recognising that he had pushed his luck as far as he should, as well as the need to be careful, he desisted and hurried back upstairs.

At one in the morning Tessa returned. Looking as vibrant and sexy as when she'd left, she walked to her door and unlocked it. With a look over her shoulder, she stepped inside and slammed the door shut.

She'd seemed a bit uneasy at the doorstep, Porter decided, as if she'd seen or heard an intruder, so he grabbed some binoculars and scanned the bushes. He was meticulous in his sweep, and it didn't look like the man was back, but he wasn't going to take any chances. He stepped into the hallway and padded downstairs. He stood in the shadows near the bushes where the skinny stalker had perched earlier to play his sick game. Well, he could be much more patient than his quarry. After all, the reward would be worth the effort.

Flies buzzed and lights flickered through the bushes. Porter could hear the distant hoots of owls as they began their nightly hunting expeditions. He was, nevertheless, struck by how quiet and still the scene had become. There was still no sign of the maintenance man.

After Tessa's lights went out Porter waited for half an hour and, seeing nothing but the resident tomcat prowl past affirming his territorial rights, he returned to his apartment. He remained vaguely aware that this situation could be a gold mine for his love life, but was at a loss as to how best to exploit it. It was time to take stock and plan.

The first thing to consider was whether the man was a serious threat? Porter knew that such people were like those with foot fetishes and exhibitionists and were not normally dangerous. They substituted the emotionally distant, and to them safer, act of watching men or women and fantasising about them for normal sexual relationships, even though they think they want the latter.

It was true, of course, that rapists would sometimes spy on their victims to learn their habits and patterns before assaulting them, but the vast majority of stalkers and watchers would never even think of speaking to their victims, much less assaulting them. The odds were that the groundsman was harmless. Besides, he was slim, and meek-looking. Tessa, with her karate training, could deck him with a single jab. No, Porter decided, there was little risk to the woman if he didn't blow the whistle on the stalker just yet. Besides, he had not yet decided what to do about Tessa himself, and he was tired.

He fell into bed and closed his eyes, but was unable to fall asleep. His brain was racing, wrestling with too many things at the same time. He tried to home in on one issue at a time, beginning with the problem of how to use the stalking man and turn his presence into a chance to ask Tessa out. Tossing from side to side uncomfortably, he beat the alarm to sleep by a mere half an hour. When it blared on at seven he stumbled out of bed and looked outside. The lights were already on in Tessa's apartment. Porter wiped the sleep from his eyes and images of her doing her morning workout or enjoying a breakfast of yoghurt and berries and herbal tea insinuated themselves into his consciousness. She was carrying on as normal, content in her ignorance of the stalker.

Porter saw not a trace of him and that was bothering. The thought struck him that the apartments may have been just a one-day assignment. He might never return, which would ruin all his plans. He remained at the window for as long as he could, hoping for him to return. But at eight, he could wait no longer. He had to do something!

Porter showered quickly and staggered outside to the car park. His head ached from the lack of sleep and his eyes stung in the fierce sunlight. He was just about to get into his battered car when a maintenance van arrived. He held his breath and watched. He was so utterly intent on what could be happening that he didn't realise he wasn't even breathing. The pain in his chest reminded him that he needed oxygen and he exhaled with a rush of air and immediately gulped a huge lungful. His head swam, but his concentration didn't waver.

Yes, it was the stalker! He climbed out, collected his tools and picked up a bag that probably contained his lunch and a drink. He headed off, followed closely and carefully by Porter, who moved behind his car and crouched down. The man slipped into the same bushes where he'd kept his vigil yesterday and started to clip a hedge that had already been perfectly trimmed. His hungry eyes didn't even glance at the clippers; they were focused on Tessa's bedroom window.

Thank you! Porter offered a prayer to any god who might exist and be listening. He hurried back to his apartment, taking the back path out of the stalker's view. He had an appointment with his dentist that day, but he couldn't forego this chance. He pulled out his mobile and made a call. He told the receptionist that he would have to make it another day. He didn't even care that it could be months in the future; there were some things that just had to take priority. He used a raspy voice and coughed hard, pretending he was not well. Perhaps that would mean a postponement of just a few days, but he received no sympathy from the other end and the phone went dead. He shrugged. He had more important things to worry about. As he walked to his apartment he was running through some of the plans he'd been thinking of as he lay in bed last night.

"Hello, you don't know me, but I live across the way. I just thought you should know...."

Or maybe: "Hi, I'm your neighbour. We haven't met and I don't want to alarm you, but there's a man in those bushes who's been staring at you for two days...."

No, don't say two days! She will only wonder why he hadn't said anything earlier.

"Listen miss, you don't know me, but don't look around. There's a man in those bushes over there, who's been staring at your apartment with some binoculars. I think he's a stalker or something."

After some debate, he decided he didn't like any of those approaches. They were too weak. She might just respond by saying, "Oh, thanks," then close the door and call the police. That would be the end of his plans. No, he needed to do something dramatic; something that would impress a woman as sleek and cool and, well, unimpressible as Tessa surely was.

Squinting into the courtyard, Porter saw that the stalker had moved closer to her apartment, eyes still focused obsessively on her window. The sunlight glinted off the blades of the clippers, which gave an ominous snap, snap. The tool was long and seemed well-honed.

He wondered if his earlier assessment had been wrong and perhaps this man really was dangerous. That thought finally gave him the idea of how to best orchestrate an introduction to the beautiful resident of number 4.

Porter rose and walked to his closet, rummaged through it and finally found an old baseball bat. He'd never been interested in sport, and he'd come across the bat in a junk shop. He bought it because he knew that in his particular line of work he would almost certainly need it one day. Besides the woman in the shop had been attractive.

A glance outside told him there was no sign of Tessa. Ominously, though the stalker was still there, clipping away fervently at thin air.

Snap, snap, snap.

Gripping the baseball bat, Porter left his apartment and slipped downstairs to the first floor path and edged quietly to the shadows behind the skinny man. His plan was to wait until Tessa left for her regular morning outing. As soon as she passed the stalker, Porter would jog up to him brandishing the bat and shout to her to call the police; this man was stalking her. He'd make the man lie face down on the pavement until they arrived. He calculated that would mean he and Tessa would have a good ten minutes to talk.

"No, no, it was nothing.....my name's Richard Porter, by the way. And you are? Nice to meet you Tessa, no, really, just being a good neighbour. Well, alright then. I'll tell you what, if you really want to repay me, you can let me take you out to dinner."

Wiping his sweating hand on his trousers, he got a firmer grip on the taped bat handle.

"Yes, Saturday would be good for me. Maybe..."

The opening front door of Tessa's apartment interrupted his fantasy. She stepped outside and pulled her expensive shades down over her eyes. Today, her black hair sported a bright red band, which matched her finger and toenail polish. She had her blue bag over her shoulder and was carrying her portfolio. She started down the walk. Porter watched, transfixed. Oh, she was lovely!

The stalker tensed and the clipping ceased. Porter gripped the bat even harder. He drew a deep breath and rehearsed his lines once more. Ready; nearly there; now!

The stalker stepped back before he could strike. He set down the clippers and began fumbling with the front of his overalls. What..? Oh, Jesus! He was unzipping himself and reaching inside. He is going to rape her!

"No!" Porter shouted and ran forward, waving the bat over his head.

"Hey!" The rapist blinked in panic and stumbled back, tripping over a small fence around a flower bed. He landed hard and cried out in pain, his breath knocked out of his lungs, gasping.

Tessa stopped, turning towards the commotion, frowning. Porter noticed that she didn't appear to understand the danger she was in. He yelled to her, "Call the police! This man's been watching you. He's a rapist!" He turned back to the blond man, waving the bat. "Don't move! I'll..."

His words were cut off by the stunning explosion of gunshots from directly behind him. Porter howled in panic and dropped to his knees as the bullets slammed into the stalker's head and neck, leaving a bloody mist around him. The man shivered once and slumped to the ground, dead.

"Christ!" Porter whispered in shock and slowly rose to his feet. He turned towards Tessa and frowned in astonishment to see her holding a large black pistol, which she'd pulled from her bag. She was crouching and looking around like a soldier in an ambush. He noticed how calm and in control she was. So she didn't just study karate for self-protection; she had a licence to carry a gun too.

Porter was mystified. Surely she hadn't just shot a man who was lying harmlessly on the ground, when he hadn't actually attacked her. Porter had the man under control; he wasn't a danger to her and now he had been blown clean away in front of his disbelieving eyes.

"Hey, you," Tessa called, stepping closer.

Porter turned. He got a good look at the woman's beautiful blue eyes and her diamond earrings sparkling in the sun, and he smelled a flowery perfume, mixed with the acrid firecracker smell of smoke from the gun.

"Me?" he asked.

■ ■

"Yes. Come here. Take this." She handed the portfolio to him.

"This is for me?"

She did not answer him. She turned away and sprinted into the alley behind the apartment block, a flash of vivacious colour that vanished an instant later. As Porter was staring in confusion at the portfolio, he heard a rustle of feet behind him and an instant later he was grabbed by half a dozen massive hands. The next thing he knew, he was being slammed face first into a patch of extremely well-raked lawn.

-22-

Tessa Goldberg, Richard Porter learned from his legal team, was one of the country's most successful, and most elusive, drug dealers. It seemed that she'd been responsible for importing thousands of kilos of high quality cocaine over the past year, which explained her frequent trips abroad. Driving a beaten up old sports car and living in a pathetic place like the apartment block kept her off the radar screen of the long arm of the law. Until now. Sitting in the interview room he learned the bad news that the powers that be had no intention of dropping any of the charges against him.

"But I didn't do anything," Porter whined.

The legal eagle, bald and annoyingly clever, chuckled as if was actually enjoying himself. Perhaps he had heard that whining line to many times. He continued by explaining that the prosecution was out for blood. Firstly, and fairly importantly, a policeman had been killed. The blond man, the apparent stalker, had actually been an undercover Drugs Squad officer, pretending to be a maintenance man. His job was to report whenever Tessa left her apartment. Other officers would then take over the surveillance and follow her in unmarked cars and vans. When Porter thought he was reaching into his trousers in preparation for a rape, the officer was merely fishing his radio out of an inside pocket to tell the surveillance team that she was leaving.

"But...""Let me finish." The bald head shone under the room's lights as he added that the police were also upset that, because of Porter's crass intervention, Tessa had successfully escaped. She'd disappeared completely and was believed to be out of the country already.

"But they can't think I was working with her! Is that what they think?"

"In a word, yes." He went on to say that Porter's explanation for the past several days' events raised eyebrows. "To put it mildly." For instance, the police were curious why, if he'd noticed the supposed stalker the day before, he hadn't told her then. If his concern, as he claimed, was for an innocent woman's safety, why didn't he tell her she was in danger when he'd first found out about it?

His red-faced explanation that he wanted to use the stalker as an excuse to introduce himself to Tessa was greeted with an expression in the lawyer's eyes that could be read as either scepticism or embarrassment for a pathetic client. The man recorded this explanation in a few disbelieving notes.

Also, why would he lie to his dentist about being sick today? To the police, that only made sense if he was serving as Tessa's lookout. Today's was to be a big drug transfer and they reasoned that Porter had stayed at home to make sure Tessa got away safely to deliver the goods. Their theory was that he had recognised the maintenance worker as a policeman and attacked him to give Tessa the chance to flee.

There was the physical evidence too: both his fingerprints and hers were on the portfolio, which happened to contain nothing but a kilo of very pure cocaine.

"She gave it to me," he'd said weakly, "to create a diversion, I'll bet. So she could escape."

The lawyer didn't even bother to write that one down.

But the most damning of all was the problem with his claim that he didn't know her.

"You see," his lawyer said, "if you really didn't know her or have any connection with her, we might get a jury to believe everything else you're claiming."

"But I really don't know her, I swear."

The lawyer gave a faint wince. "Unfortunately, we have a problem there."

"A problem?"

"They searched your apartment."

"Oh. They did? Can they do that?"

That was met with a laugh. "You were arrested for murder, assault, aiding and abetting and drug charges. Yes, Richard, they can do that."

"Oh."

"And do you know what they found?" The lawyer persisted.

He knew perfectly well what they found. He sat back, stared at the floor and played absently with the handcuffs as the lawyer read from a sheet of paper.

"Some old yoghurt cartons with Tessa's fingerprints on them. The same for two wine bottles, a box of herbal tea and empty strawberry cartons. Magazines with her name on the address label. A debit card receipt of hers from a local supermarket, a coffee carton with her lipstick and DNA on the rim."

"DNA? They checked that, did they?"

"That's what police do, I'm afraid."

"I swear, she was never in my apartment. All that stuff....I just....I kind of....picked it up in her rubbish."

"Her rubbish?"

"I just saw some things out behind her apartment. I didn't think it was a big deal."

"You had two dozen pictures of her in various places."

"I just took a few, that's all. She wasn't looking at the camera, you can tell the police that. If I really knew her, she'd have been looking at the camera, wouldn't she?"

"Richard. Please, I want to help you, but you've got to be realistic."

"No, listen!" If we had been together somewhere she'd be looking at me, looking into the lens."

Porter's voice broke in desperation. "But she wasn't. That means we weren't together. It's just logic. Doesn't that make sense?" He fell silent. After a minute he added, "I just wanted to meet her, I don't know how."

"They found some binoculars too. They figured you used those to keep an eye on her door to warn her if anybody was going to raid her place."

"That was just so I could.....so I could look at her. She's really pretty." Porter shrugged and his eyes returned to the floor.

"I think the only thing we can do is talk to the about a plea bargain. We don't want to go to trial on this one, believe me. I may be able to get you a deal for fifteen, maybe twenty years..."

"Twenty years?"

"I'll talk to them. See what they say."

The lawyer stepped to the door of the interview room and rapped on it to summon the guard. A moment later it opened.

"One thing," Porter said.

"What's that?" The lawyer turned and lifted an eyebrow.

"Lisa Richards."

"Who?"

"I did a job for her once. A contract and then we went out and it lasted for some time. It finished eventually, of course. They all do. I can't seem to maintain a relationship. The same sort of thing happened with her."

"Same thing?"

"Like with Tessa. I was kind of watching her more than I should have."

"Stalking?"

He started to object to the word, but then nodded.

"After we finished I couldn't let go. I got arrested. That's why I moved here. I wanted to start again and meet somebody for real."

"What was your sentence?"

"Six months, suspended and a year's counselling."

"That didn't work, did it?"

"No, it doesn't seem so," Porter sighed.

"I'll get the records. They might buy it. But they lost a prime suspect because of you, so they're going to want their pound of flesh. Probably stalking and privacy charges. You'd have to do a year, eighteen months I'd guess."

"Better than twenty," Porter said.

"I'll see what I can do." The lawyer stepped through the door.

"One other question?" Porter asked, looking up.

"What?"

The prisoner said, "Will the police use all of those things they found? For evidence?"

"From your apartment? Probably not. They usually pick the best ones."

"Then do you think I could have a couple of the pictures of Tessa to put on my wall? There's nothing to look at in a cell."

The lawyer hesitated, as if Porter was joking. When he concluded that apparently the prisoner wasn't, he said, "You know, Quentin, that's probably not the best idea in the world."

"Just a thought. How did you know?" Quentin Legard asked.

"It's my job," the lawyer said, as a large guard stepped inside. He took the prisoner by the arm and led him to the corridor that would take him back to his cell.

FREE TO FLY
-23-

"Very interesting," said Frank into the phone.

"Yes. I didn't think he was going to confess. Though I'm not so sure he has made a completely clean breast of it, but there is another consideration."

"Oh, that also sounds interesting," said Frank.

"Indeed it is," replied the voice. "I was summoned to a meeting in London. The Boss from Hereford, a stuffed shirt from Whitehall and myself. I can't go into details, but the upshot is that we are going to allow Quentin Legard to run free. We are certain he will recommence his criminal activities. The powers that be are interested in the people he contacts and they want them eliminated. The plan is to use Legard to do their work for them. When it's over, we'll reel him in and his day of reckoning will come. I have made an arrangement with them."

"I trust it is to your satisfaction," said Frank.

"Oh yes," the voice replied.

"Care to enlighten me?" asked Frank, fishing for his own interest.

"Listen," commanded the voice, "make no comment. Legard must not know what is happening."

"Ok," agreed Frank.

"We are certain Legard won't be able to help himself. He knows only one way of life and has absolutely no scruples or morals. We think we know what he'll get himself involved with and he will be watched. There are characters that we know he will contact who need to be eliminated. He is being given enough rope with which to finally hang himself. It has to be done this way; there is far too much openness these days and it's not the time for publicity."

"Intriguing," offered Frank.

"Also, I have another reason to be involved. I'm bored," said the voice.

Frank knew that if the man on the other end of the phone was bored, then he was a very dangerous individual indeed.

"Oh, I see," he said, keeping his promise to ensure Legard was unable to understand.

"I'm bored," the voice reiterated, "I need to do something active. I don't want to hang around my wife's damned horses for the rest of my natural. You know how it is in our line of work. Once you're in; you're in for life."

"I understand," said Frank.

The man on the other end of the line had omitted to tell Frank another aspect of the situation, but Frank knew the details without having to ask. For the man on the other end it was personal.

"It's been agreed that once the appropriate moment arrives I shall intervene and Quentin Legard will be left to my tender care. No questions will be asked."

"The poor bugger," said Frank, with feeling.

"I'll still need your help," the voice at the other end was firm and definite.

"You don't have to ask. Just tell me what you want," said Frank.

The voice gave a detailed plan and finished by saying, "carry on, if you don't mind. I want him absolutely ready to meet me."

"It's my pleasure," said Frank.

He set his phone down and turned to go back to address his confused student. Quentin Legard had only heard Frank's end of the conversation, so could only guess what was happening. Frank had been deliberately careful to ensure he gave little away, but also knew Legard had been given sufficient to pique his interest and raise his hopes.

"It seems that you have a guardian angel," Frank said to Legard.

"Sorry, what do you mean?" Quentin asked, mystified.

"You obviously know that somebody else has been watching you whilst you watched that film."

"I had my suspicions," said Legard.

"Well, it was more than one person. It was three actually, and by a majority verdict they have decided that you have shown enough contrition. For some reason they believe you have learned your lesson and are prepared to give you the benefit of the doubt," Frank explained.

""What does that mean?" asked Legard, not allowing himself to show elation.

"It means, Mr Legard that you are free to go. I've been instructed to set you free. I may have played the part of a priest, but you'd better be very careful to avoid me in future. I'm not a forgiving man in real life." Frank's words were deliberate.

"Don't worry, once I leave here, you won't see me again," Legard promised, unable to believe or understand his fortune.

"Before you go," Frank said, "you need to know something."

"What's that?" asked Legard.

"A warning. If you take up your criminal ways again, you will be found out. I won't be able to save you and nor would I wish to."

Frank paused and looked at the man in front of him. Legard couldn't fathom whether he was receiving pity or being given hope.

"There are people higher up than me, people with far greater power and influence, who will find you and then you'll wish you'd never been born. Believe me," Frank paused again, "these are people that scare me, so they'll certainly frighten you."

-24-

When you've been an opportunist for as long as you can remember; when you've lived by your wits, probably since you could walk, then you know when something is there for you. You sense it; you can smell it. It was happening to Chris. He was watching two men on the other side of the room, leaning at the bar. Neither of them looked particularly happy. They hardly talked to each other or, indeed, anybody else. They simply sipped their drinks, with increasing frequency and blinked like lizards. Chris had seen one of them in the pub, The Grapes of Wrath, before. He was wearing a suit and tie, which was unusual for that particular public house. His companion was dressed in a manner which was more normal. He had a leather jacket, jeans and designer footwear. He was obviously not a happy young man because he shook his head at everything the suited man was telling him. He even slammed his fist on the bar so hard that the glasses bounced in reaction to something that was said. Despite the sudden noise, nobody noticed and that summed up The Grapes of Wrath. Customers didn't interfere with anybody else's business. The world was better that way.

Chris was in his usual place, sat at the end of the bar, on his customary stool. The barman, who always knew exactly what was going on but never seemed to take notice of anything, kept a wary eye and an attentive ear on the argument. From that point of view, he was an excellent barman.

"It's alright," Chris told him, "I'm watching it."

The man in the suit had opened a case, to show a collection of papers inside. It was not normal for a case with papers to be on such open display in that place. The usual trade consisted of pungent plants and cases of whisky and cigarettes, and even then business was always conducted in the alley at the back of the pub, with an attentive lookout in position. Chris, being the sharp operator he was, concluded this was something different. His opportunist's eye, his reliable sixth sense, told him to pay attention.

"No way. No chance," said the character in the leather jacket.

"Sorry." The suited man was obviously a man of few words.

"You've said that before, but you don't really sound sorry. Perhaps that's because I'm the one who's lost all the money." His designer trainers were tapping, agitated, against the side of the bar.

Chris's interest was piqued. He had long ago learned that other people losing money doesn't take the sting out of you losing money. It was the way of the world. It was just the way things went. The leather jacketed man was becoming more and more agitated. He looked around before hissing, "Listen here, my friend. I'll make some phone calls. I know some people down there, but you won't want to mess with those people."

The suited man tapped what looked like a newspaper article in the case.

"Just what do you think you can do?" he challenged. He lowered his voice and whispered something that obviously upset the other man. "Now, just go home like a good boy, and keep your head down. You'd better pray they can't..."

Chris couldn't make out the rest because somebody else in the bar laughed loudly. He snorted with annoyance because he would have very much liked to know what 'they' might do.

"This is not over, you prick!" shouted the man in the leather jacket, smashing his fist on the bar.

Heads turned. Normality had been disturbed; an unwritten code of practice broken.

"Gentlemen, please, let's have some decorum. Don't disturb the punters." Chris intervened. The barman smiled his gratitude.

"Who the hell are you, little man?" demanded the angry man, glaring with red-faced anger.

His suited companion touched his arm to calm him, but he pulled away and began to rise from his stool. Chris eased off his own stool, brushed back his greasy hair and walked to the front of the bar. His boots clicked loudly on the floor. The angry man was many inches taller than Chris and much heavier, but Chris had learned long ago that people are afraid of others who are crazy. He therefore made his eyes gleam weirdly, got right into the man's face and screamed, "I'll tell you who I am. I'm your worst nightmare. I'm the one person you didn't want to meet. You need to get out of here now, before I lose my temper."

"Piss off, you little prick," the man spat.

Chris didn't move. He just grinned and let the other man start to imagine what was about to happen. A few seconds passed. Finally, the angry man drank what was left of his beer with a shaking hand and, attempting to hold on to what little dignity he had left, he strolled to the door laughing and muttering.

"I'm sorry about that," said the man in the suit. He dug in his pocket and produced money for the drinks as he made to leave.

"You stay there," Chris commanded. He looked into the case and saw pictures of expensive looking, top of the range vehicles. "Sorry, I didn't mean to shout at you. Please, stay. It's just that I like to keep things calm and peaceful here, you know."

The man noticed Chris looking into his case and closed it quickly. "Is this your place?" he asked.

Chris looked up and saw that the barman was out of earshot. "More or less," he replied. "So, did that man lose some money?"

"It was just a business deal that didn't work out," the man replied.

"How much did he lose?" Chris asked.

"I don't really know," answered the man.

"Let me buy you a beer," offered Chris. "I'm sorry, but I don't understand. You're in business with him and you don't know how much money he lost."

"What I don't understand," said the man," is why I should tell you."

Chris allowed the tension of the moment to develop before laughing. "No problems. It's none of my business."

The beers arrived on the bar in front of them, and they introduced themselves.

"Chris Newton."

"Bob Carter."

"I'm sure I've seen you before," said Chris. "Do you live round here?"

"No, I come here on business from time to time. That's probably when you've seen me."

"What about you?" Bob asked.

"I've got a place here," said Chris. He failed to mention that it actually belonged to a man he knew as JB.

"Those cars," said Chris, nodding towards the case. "Is that your line of business?"

"Yes, along with a few other things. What about you?" Bob asked.

"Oh, I get by," Chris preferred to concentrate on his new friend rather than divulging his own information. I do all sorts of things. I am always on the lookout for opportunities to keep the wolf from the door. I've got a sharp eye."

"I see," said Bob. "What does your sharp eye tell you at the moment?"

"That I have just met a chancer," replied Chris, evenly.

Bob was affronted. He didn't particularly take to being labelled as a chancer.

"Why do you think that?" Bob asked.

"It's obvious," stated Chris. "You did not come here to sell some mug a car. Why not tell me what it's really all about?"

"There's nothing to tell. A business deal didn't work out. It happens, and I'm not going to lose any sleep over it."

"Oh, come on," said Chris, "it was a scam if ever I saw one. How does it work?"

"I beg your pardon!" exclaimed Bob, "it was not a scam. I resent that allegation."

"You can resent what you like," replied Chris, "but I know a scam when I see one. You can't kid a kidder, you know."

"It was not a con. I was going to sell him a car. It didn't work out. There's no more to it than that."

"Have it your way," said Chris, "but let me tell you what I think.

"Go ahead, be my guest," said Bob, appearing unworried.

"I've seen people upset many times, but that man was not annoyed about not getting a car. He was angry about not getting his deposit back. Don't answer that, I know I'm right. The question is why didn't he get his money back?" Chris was drilling into the heart of the matter.

Bob shrugged and said nothing, but Chris took this as a sign that he was on the right track and he ploughed on.

Let me put forward a theory," he said. "You borrow a car, sell it to somebody, but on the way here it has an accident. There's nothing he can do about it. He loses his deposit and it's just bad luck. He won't complain to anybody because it's a stolen car."

Bob shrugged again and still remained silent.

"To continue," said Chris, "The point is that there never was any car because you only showed him pictures. Oh, and I would imagine you show him a fake police report or something. That's a neat touch. It adds authenticity."

Bob finally laughed, but made no other reaction.

"The only risk for you is that your victim might go to the police, but I doubt it. It's a clever con. Congratulations."

Bob didn't deny the accusation, and that was what confirmed it to Chris. He tried a different approach.

"Alright, so you sell cars. That means you're always in need of buyers. I could find one for you." Chris made the offer and stopped to study the response.

"Do you know somebody who's interested in cars?" Bob asked.

"I know lots of people. I have many contacts around here. Some of them are interested in cars." Chris was reeling him in.

"Alright," Bob leaned in closer to Chris and lowered his voice. "I'll tell you about it, but if you've got an idea about going to the police, you'd better think twice. I too have friends and if you cross me, they'll find you and you seriously don't want to wish that on yourself. Some of them have a strange addiction to inflicting pain and they prefer to do it slowly. So, think on. Also, what I'm doing may not be exactly legal in the strict senses of the word, but I'm hardly murdering anybody or peddling Class A drugs am I? So, even if you go to the police they'll take your statement and send you on your way. With the lack of resources they've got at the moment, it'll be at the bottom of the pile and, eventually, go so cold that it will never see the light of day. You'll have wasted your time." Bob ended his longest speech yet with a grin.

"Don't worry. I'm no grass. All I want to do is make some money and my sharp eye tells me that an opportunity has arisen." Chris ignored the warning and hoped the appeal of doing business would reel this man in further.

"I don't want deposits," said Bob. "The buyer pays everything up front, no matter how much that is. The buyer is told that I have connections who know where confiscated cars are kept. That part is true. The cars are kept for a short while and then either crushed or sold at auction. The problem is that these days there are so many of them that they don't all get logged in when they should. I tell the buyer my connection is breaking into the pound early in the morning, loading up a car on a transporter, or just driving it away before it's got an official record. We move it far away, stick a new registration on it, get rid of the number on the engine block, and that's it. For less than half the proper price, the buyer has himself an expensive top of the range car. I even take orders, if a buyer has a preference for a particular make or model, but that can take longer and I might put on an extra charge because of the additional bother."

Chris listened intently and seemed interested.

"Then," Bob went on," after I get the money, I break the bad news. You heard that earlier. Also I show them a newspaper report about theft from police car pounds. It talks about arrests and the recovery of a lot of money. Buyers are named and shamed as well."

"Now that's clever," Chris was genuinely impressed by that touch. "You print the paper yourself, have it in your case and show the buyer so that he won't go to the police for fear of being exposed himself."

"Well, nobody wants to be made to look a fool in public, do they?" Bob asked, grinning broadly.

"It's brilliant, I think we could do business." Chris seemed keen. "If I find you a buyer, what's in it for me?

Bob stared ahead. "I don't need anybody to find buyers, you know. I'm doing fine as I am."

"I'm sure you're always open to making more money," Chris smiled. "Besides, it could be the beginning of a beautiful friendship."

"Oh, well, let's say twenty five percent," Bob said.

"Let's not," returned Chris. "I think fifty is more like it."

"I'll give you twenty five percent if the buyer pays fifty thousand or less.   Anything over that and you get thirty percent." Bob was used to bargaining.

"No, if it's over fifty thousand, then I want half," Chris had also been brought up in the school of hard knocks.

Bob sat and pretended to think. He took his time, as if he were wrestling with an insoluble difficulty.

"Oh, what the hell? We have a deal," he said and offered his hand. "Do you really know somebody with that kind of money?"

Chris finished his beer and, without paying, started for the door. "That's exactly where I'm going now."

-25-

Chris walked from The Grapes of Wrath to the King's Head, which took him about fifteen minutes. It was a busier pub and had a different clientele. It was close to hotels and conference centres and people often spilled out of those places and made for the King's Head. It served good pub food and proper ale. It also served as a meeting place for those attending conferences who wanted some discreet extra- curricular activity. It sat in an expensive and thriving area.

JB sat at a corner table. Although he owned the Grapes of Wrath he preferred to drink at the King's Head sometimes. He had designs on purchasing the place at some time in the future and could often be found scoping it out; doing his homework like every good businessman should. The other draw was the particularly attractive women who could always be found frequenting the establishment. A lot of them were of the professional variety and they could be easily identified as they arrived alone and left accompanied very shortly afterwards. JB was more interested in the equally attractive women who were obviously attending conferences and were in town for a night or two. They usually arrived in groups. They often left accompanied, but that took longer and a few more drinks to accomplish.

JB was the centre of attention at his table which was laden with the evidence of a hard night's drinking.

"Hey, Chris!" JB called. He was not drunk but not sober either. It was his usual state.

"Hey," Chris called in return.

"Where have you been?" JB asked, looking round, grinning at his three drinking partners.

"Your place," Chris replied.

"What for? It's much better here. Look around you," JB was goading him.

Chris didn't rise to the bait. He knew if he agreed, JB would turn the tables and get angry about his disrespect for the pub he owned. He fetched a pint of Guinness and sat down. He watched as JB held court and insulted everyone there in turn in his inimitable not drunk, not sober style.

Then the door swung open and a stranger walked in. He was about fifty years old and wore expensive clothes. There was a lanyard around his neck from which hung a badge. Chris couldn't see what it said from a distance, but it was obviously an entry pass to a conference. Chris shook his head in disgust because the man had obviously kept it round his neck as a badge of invitation. It said, 'I'm in town for a couple of nights, there's money in my pocket and I'm looking for action."

Chris supped his Guinness and started work on a plan to transfer some of that money to his own pocket. The newcomer wore a Rolex and the closer he got Chris identified it as genuine. His clothes were designer labels from head to toe. The man surveyed the pub, slowly looking around, and it reminded Chris of the way people looked at animals at the zoo. Chris dismissed the notion of simply mugging the man outside. He and JB had done that before, of course, but only when really necessary. It was just not worth the bother. If a stranger got hurt he would probably go to the police, but if a stranger was more subtly relieved of money, he would more often than not, keep quiet. After all, he didn't want to explain his presence in such a place to his family and colleagues and be made to look an idiot or worse. For Chris, there were better ways that required much less effort. JB looked at Chris and caught his eye. He nodded. No more words were necessary.

The man sat a table. He had a bottle of wine in front of him. He took a drink and Chris looked at his hand. He was pleased to spot not only the genuine Rolex, but also a gold ring, with a large diamond on it.

"I think this is your lucky day," thought Chris, "and mine."

Within half an hour Chris and the man from out of town were standing in the grimy entrance hall of a local guest house. Chris introduced the man.

"This is Lola," he said.

"Hello, Lola." The man had manners as well as money, thought Chris.

"What's your name?" she asked, almost whispering in her effort to be husky.

"Umm, Jack."

Chris almost choked as he realised the man had almost given his name as John.

· ·

"It's nice to meet you, Jack," Lola said. She was almost six feet tall, beautiful and built for her present occupation. She had also been a man until three years ago. The out of town stranger didn't realise this, or perhaps he did. Either way, he was there for the taking; eager and helpless. Jack checked them into a room and paid for three hours. Chris was impressed. Three hours! The man had stamina, style and ambition.

-26-

Detective Constable Martin Shelvey had been a detective for nearly twenty years. He was a man who began his career with praiseworthy morals, but had increasingly felt undervalued and, more particularly, underpaid. He walked down a dirty corridor with his partner, who pointed at a door.

"That's it," he said.

The two officers listened intently, straining to hear any noises from within. There was no sound and Shelvey pulled out a master key, unlocked the door and pushed inside, with his partner in his wake.

"Police. Don't move. Stay where you are!" He shouted.

The faces of the two people inside registered identical expressions of shock, which turned quickly to horror and dismay. The man had a regimental tattoo on his arm and had probably been tough in his younger days, but had now turned to fat. His narrow' pale shoulders slumped and he looked on the verge of tears.

"No, no, no......"

"Oh, Shit," Lola said.

"Stay where you are, both of you."

"How the hell did you find me?" asked the man.

"Oh Lord," Lola groaned. She looked at Shelvey's partner with a withering gaze, but he just laughed and put her in handcuffs.

Shelvey addressed the man. "Have you any ID on you, please?" he demanded. He could afford to be polite. It cost nothing, after all, and often had the desired effect.

"Please, officer; look, I didn't…"

"Please, sir, don't waste my time."

The man dug out his thick wallet from his trouser pocket and handed it to Shelvey.

"Is this your current address?" asked the officer.

"Yes, yes, it is," the man replied in a quivering voice.

"Alright. I'm arresting you for solicitation of a prostitute."

"I didn't do anything illegal. It was just….it was only a date."

Detective Shelvey picked up a pile of money from the dusty bedside table. He counted four hundred pounds.

"I just thought….I…."

He could literally see the stranger's mind working overtime. Shelvey waited, wondering what excuse he'd come up with. He had heard them all, but was always willing to add to the collection.

"Just to get some food and something to drink."

Success! It was a new excuse and Shelvey tried hard not to laugh. You could spend all that on food and drink and still have change for a few Lolas.

"Did he pay you to have sex?" Shelvey asked Lola.

She pulled a face.

"Come on, don't make this difficult. If you lie you know what will happen to you. If you're honest, I'll put in a good word for you."

"Lola snapped. "Alright, he paid me for it."

"No..." The stranger protested for a moment but then he gave up and slumped even lower. "Oh God, what have I done? What am I going to do? This will kill my wife and my kids." He looked up with panic in his eyes. "Will I have to go to court or jail?"

"That depends," said Shelvey. He then looked at Lola carefully. "Take her downstairs," he said to his partner.

"Woah! You keep your hands off me," Lola shouted.

Shelvey's partner laughed. "Oh, I suppose this means you're not my girlfriend anymore?" He gripped Lola by the arm and led her outside.

"Please, Detective. Can't we talk about this? It's not like I robbed anybody, you know. It's victimless. Yes, that's it: victimless." The out of town man was desperate.

"A crime is a crime," Shelvey told the man. "I can't pick and choose which ones I let go and which I don't. Anyway, didn't you mother tell you about AIDS or hepatitis?" He couldn't resist patronising.

"Look, I know it's a crime, but for heaven's sake, it's pretty low level. And, for your information, Detective, I know about the risks." The man couldn't resist returning the compliment with his own sarcasm.

Detective Shelvey still held the handcuffs. He decided he was tired and sat on a creaky chair. The guilty man had already noticed that he wasn't yet in handcuffs and he took that, as well as the officer sitting down, as a hopeful sign. If the officer was going to arrest him, surely he would already be in handcuffs.

"How often do you come to London?" he asked.

"Once a year. I attend the same conference each year. I quite enjoy it. I get to catch up with old friends and make new ones."

"You also take the opportunity to play away," commented Detective Shelvey.

"Well, it's harmless. Nobody gets hurt. Besides you know what they say, 'it's a nice place to visit, but you wouldn't want to live there.' Oh, I'm sorry, I didn't mean to offend." His voice tailed off and he stopped before he did any more damage.

"Detective Shelvey said, "Are you attending the conference now?" He pulled the badge from the man's pocket and read it.

"Yes, I am," replied the man. He was slowly gaining confidence, but was trying not to give the officer any reason to arrest him and let due process take its inexorable course. He knew it would only have one outcome, and he dreaded that. It was a fine balancing act.

"I take it you run your own business." It was not a question and the man realised it immediately.

"Yes," he said, wary now.

Detective Shelvey nodded slowly and eventually put the handcuffs away. The out of town man breathed a sigh to himself and his eyes narrowed. He had a strange feeling that he knew which way it was heading.

"Have you ever done anything like this before, Jack?" Shelvey asked. He emphasised the name.

"Yes," said the man, trying to ignore the insult.

"I'm sure you won't be doing it again, will you?" asked the officer.

Jack blinked and lowered his head, showing what he hoped was the correct amount of contrition. "Never. You can rely on that."

Shelvey allowed a long pause to develop before ordering the man to stand. Jack obeyed and was startled to find himself being frisked as the officer searched for listening devices or weapons. Satisfied, he was told to sit again with a cursory nod of Shelvey's head.

"Sorry. I had to make sure. I can't afford any mistakes now," explained the policeman. "Now, I have a proposition for you."

Jack was wary. "Proposition?"

"Yes. A proposition. I'm fairly convinced you won't do this again, so I could let you off with a warning."

"That sounds fair," said Jack, eager to snatch at the unexpected opportunity. He had been worried that the situation might cost him a good deal of money.

"However, there is one problem," said Shelvey.

Here we go, Jack thought to himself. "Problem?" he asked.

"Yes," replied the detective. "The situation has already been reported. A plain clothes officer working with the Vice Squad happened to see you go into the guest house with Lola. She's known to us, you see and the premises were being watched as well. I got sent here because of his report. I'm afraid there's already a record about the incident."

"My name?" Jack asked.

"No, just a suspect at the moment. But there is a report. I could make it disappear, but it would take some work and it would be risky." Detective Shelvey had begun his pitch.

Jack sighed, nodding as he recognised the inevitable, and opened the bidding. It wasn't much of an auction. Jack volunteered figures and Shelvey just kept raising his thumb to indicate that he wanted more. There had to be an acceptable figure, Jack knew, but it was getting ridiculous. Finally, when the sum arrived at £150,000, Shelvey nodded and kept his thumb still.

"Bloody hell," was all Jack could muster.

It was JB and Chris who had set it up. They had called Detective Shelvey and told him they had a tourist to target and that he could be good for a six figure score.

In a defeated voice Jack asked, "can I give you a cheque?"

Shelvey laughed and didn't even bother to answer.

"Alright, but I'll need some time. I can't get hold of that sort of money just like that," he said, snapping his fingers.

"I expected that," Shelvey replied. "Shall we say tonight at eight?" The question was rhetorical.

A meeting place was arranged. "I'll keep your driving licence and the evidence," said Shelvey as he picked up the cash from the table. "If you don't show, your feet won't touch. There'll be an arrest warrant and you'll be in a cell quicker than you can even imagine."

"Don't worry, I'll get the money. Every penny," promised Jack as he dressed as rapidly as he could.

"You'd better use the service door at the back; I don't know where the Vice Squad officer is," Shelvey advised.

The tourist nodded and scuttled away as fast as his legs could carry him. In the entrance hall next to the lift, the detective found his partner and Lola sharing a cigarette directly beneath a large 'no smoking' sign.

"Where's my money?" Lola demanded.

Shelvey handed her two hundred of the confiscated cash. He gave his partner fifty and kept the rest for himself. The division indicated what he considered to be the importance of each of them in the ruse.

"Perhaps you should take the afternoon off," suggested his partner.

"No way," she replied. I have to work. Now, if you paid me the same for not doing my work as I get for actually doing it, I'll gladly take some time off." Her logic was impeccable.

Shelvey snorted and walked away.

When he walked into the pub the course of at least half of the conversations changed abruptly. He was known as a crooked policeman, but he was, nevertheless, still an officer of the law. Talk moved from deals, scams and drugs to sport, women and jobs. Shelvey laughed and strode across the room. He sat heavily in an empty chair at the heavily stained table and demanded a beer from JB. It wasn't a request; it was more like an order and he was the only person in the pub who could get away with the disrespect.

"He was a good one," he said, as he lifted his glass in acknowledgement to Chris. "He agreed to one hundred and fifty."

"Well, well," JB said, lifting an eyebrow. The split had already been agreed. Shelvey had half and JB and Chris divided the rest equally, or however they decided between themselves. That part was not Shelvey's business.

"So, where's he getting it from? asked JB.

"I wouldn't know," replied Shelvey. "It's not my problem, it's his."

Chris looked up. "Hold on. I want the watch as well. He had a Rolex, and I want it."

■ ı

Shelvey already had at least a dozen Rolexes that he had confiscated over the years and didn't feel he needed another one.

"No problem," the detective said. "If you want it, then you shall have it. Your wish is my command," he mocked as he waved his hand in regal fashion. "He won't worry about a watch. All he's concerned with is making sure his wife and colleagues don't find out what he's been up to."

"No way," JB was there in an instant. "I get first option on the watch."

"Never," said Chris. "It's my tourist, so I get the watch."

"Give it a rest," Shelvey interrupted. "You two are like little schoolchildren. We'll sort that out later. He'll meet us at eight tonight."

The three men had carried out the same scam, or variations of it, for a couple of years, but they still didn't completely trust each other. Therefore they would all go to the meeting at eight.

Shelvey drained the last of his beer. "See you two tonight. Don't be late or I might take it all," he threatened.

Chris and JB both knew it wasn't an empty promise.

After a while Chris rose and announced, "I'm going out for a while."

-27-

Detective Shelvey had walked a beat earlier in his career. He'd investigated hundreds of crimes and been part of even more scams. All of which meant that he'd learned how to stay alive on the streets.

"Have you recognised yourself yet," Frank asked Quentin.

Legard shook his head. His whole body ached as a result of being strapped upright to the wooden palette. His neck was particularly sore as he tried to see what was written on the screen.

"Never mind. Just keep concentrating. All will become clear shortly," said Frank. "Let's continue."

The script on the screen said that Shelvey sensed a threat. A weird scraping could be heard. Somebody was behind him. He paused in a doorway and looked to see the reflection in a shop window. Just as he thought, he saw a man in a cheap grey suit, wearing gloves, about thirty feet behind him. The man paused for a moment and pretended to look into a different shop window. Shelvey did not recognise him. He knew he'd made many enemies over the years and some of them might hold grudges. It only took one and there were plenty of strange people out there.

He continued walking, forcing himself to concentrate all of his senses on the matter at hand. He heard more scraping shoes behind him. He thought they belonged to only one pair of feet, but he couldn't be sure. He used the rear-view mirror of a car which was parked nearby, which told him the man was getting closer now. He saw that his hands were at his side and not in any pocket, which would have indicated him reaching for a weapon. Shelvey found his mobile and fished it from his pocket. He pretended to make a call. This was an excuse to slow down without making the man behind suspicious. People often slow down when talking on their mobile phones because they concentrate on the call rather than what they had been doing. Shelvey knew that, just as he knew it also happened when people used mobile phones in cars. Their attention tended to be on the call rather than on the primary function of driving. Accidents happened and people died for that reason. Despite that, and it also being illegal apart from hand free sets, people still did it. The mobile phone had become increasingly important, and, for some, it had taken over their lives.

Shelvey's other hand slipped inside his coat as a warning, but the man did not stop this time.

"Please stop your call, detective."

Shelvey blinked and turned round. His pursuer was holding a badge in his outstretched hand. Shelvey recognised it immediately as from Internal Affairs, the department that investigated corrupt policemen. He knew they took no prisoners, and reprimanded himself for the unintended pun.

"What are you doing following me?" Shelvey demanded, knowing that it was important to be on the front foot.

"I'd like to ask you a few questions." The reply was brief and to the point.

"What's this all about?" Shelvey pressed on, as if he had not heard what the man had said.

"An investigation we're conducting." The man was being deliberately obtuse.

"Excuse me, I think I've already worked that out for myself," Shelvey's voice dripped with sarcasm.

The other man remained silent.

"For heaven's sake, let's have some details!" exploded Shelvey.

The other man sighed and said, "we're looking into your connection with certain individuals."

Detective Shelvey was exasperated. "You don't have to talk like a policeman, you know. It's not compulsory. 'Certain individuals' indeed," he mocked.

This time there was no response, so Shelvey had no choice but to continue.

"I have 'connections' as you call it with a lot of people. Perhaps you're thinking of my snouts. I have to see them sometimes. It's part of the job. I wouldn't get results otherwise. They give me information. It's what it's all about." Shelvey was annoyed with this man and his impertinence.

"I'll need your warrant card," the man said, showing no emotion whatsoever.

"Piss off," Shelvey hissed.

"Look, I'm trying to make this easy for you. It's the easy way or the hard way; your choice. If you don't co-operate, I'll arrest you and take you in. Then it will all be out there for all to see and paw over."

The penny dropped at last. He was being scammed, by Internal Affairs no less. So they were on the take too. Ironic.

"I won't give you my warrant card, but you obviously want to talk, so let's go somewhere less public," suggested Shelvey. He wondered how much it was going to cost him.

"That way," Internal Affairs said, nodding towards the riverbank.

"Come on, talk to me," Shelvey said. "I've got a right to know what this is all about. If somebody's told you I'm bent, it's rubbish. Whoever told you that has an angle himself."

Shelvey was sounding off, deliberately angry. It was all part of the negotiation, he knew. It was much like the initial stages of courtship, he thought. Each person assessing the situation, making certain moves, giving out particular signals just to get a response. The spiral continuing until a decision was made by either or both parties.

They came to the entrance of a long, dark and narrow alleyway. Suddenly, the man stopped in his tracks, turned and shoved Shelvey into the blackness. He was taken off guard. It was a momentary and uncharacteristic lapse.

"Ok, listen," shouted Shelvey. "I've got money. Whatever you're being paid to do this, I'll pay more."

"Shut up!"

Shelvey felt the unmistakable sting of the tip of a sharp blade, and the warm trickle of his own blood. The fake officer pulled a piece of paper out of his pocket and stuffed it into Detective Shelvey's own pocket. He leaned forward and whispered, with undisguised menace, "here's the message. For two years JB's been setting up everything, doing all the work and you've been taking half the money. You've messed with the wrong man for long enough."

"That's nonsense," Shelvey cried in desperation. "He needs me as much as I need him. He couldn't do it without me."

"Goodbye," said the man as he moved the knife round to the front of Shelvey's throat and held the razor sharp blade against his shaking skin.

"You don't need to do this," Shelvey whispered. "You really don't. Please, listen. Let's talk. I'm sure we can work something out."

Then it happened. A scream sounded from the mouth of the alley.

"Oh my God!" A woman stood less than thirty feet away, staring at the scene. The knife glinted as it caught a light, and she saw it was held against the throat of one of the men. "Help! Help! Somebody call the police," she yelled.

The knifeman was distracted for a split second, but it was enough. Shelvey shoved him into a brick wall and ran down the alley as fast as his legs would carry him.

"Oh, shit!" the other man shouted as he took after his quarry.

Shelvey was on home ground and the other man stood no chance once they entered the intricate maze of side streets and back alleys. It took him less than five minutes to lose his man. Once he was sure he had time and was alone, he felt the crinkle of paper in his pocket. He withdrew it and was shocked. It was a fake suicide note; Shelvey's note confessing that he'd been bent and on the take for years and couldn't stand the guilt anymore. He had to end it all. He decided that the note was correct. Something was about to end.

He made his way to the pub and waited in the shadows. He was prepared to wait for as long as it took. It didn't matter to Shelvey; a line had been crossed. Fifteen minutes later JB emerged alone. He looked around, checking that he was not being followed. It was an old habit, ingrained by lessons learned long ago. He failed to spot Shelvey, who let him have some distance and then fell into step behind him. He matched his stride so that their footsteps hit the floor at the same. It was an old trick, but useful nonetheless. He felt in his coat pocket for his weapon. He wrapped his fingers around it and found it reassuring. Not for him the noise and bloody mess of a gun; not for him the sharp blade that could also cut himself. He preferred his length of thin nylon twine and his trusty pencil.

He quickly gained ground on JB. He told himself not to talk to his victim. He remembered an old film he'd once seen in which the killer feels the need to talk to his victim to explain why he's about to die. The victim had just drawn a gun and shot the would-be killer between the eyes, saying as he did so, "If you're going to kill just get on with it. Kill don't talk." Detective Shelvey followed the dictum to the letter. JB must have heard him because he started to turn, but before he even caught sight of his partner of many scams, Shelvey slipped the twine noose over his head and drew it tightly around his neck. He inserted his pencil between the twine and JB's neck and twisted it. It tightened quickly, choking off any sound or protest and it wasn't long before JB's body went slack. Shelvey maintained the pressure until he was certain JB had drawn his final breath and then let his body fall to the ground.

He walked to the river and let the twine and pencil float gently away with the current. He kept his head down as he walked away.

"No talking to the victim. Just do it. Amen to that," he muttered to himself.

He walked with a purpose. He needed to see Chris. He wanted to see his reaction when he arrived instead of JB. He was sure as soon as Chris returned his gaze. Shelvey knew Chris was not involved. He didn't show any hint of surprise that the detective was still alive. Shelvey's experience of interviewing countless suspects over the years told him that this one knew nothing about JB's attempted treachery.

Chris nodded, "where's JB?" he asked, looking around. "He said he'd be here early."

Shelvey frowned. "Haven't you heard?"

"Heard what?" asked Chris.

"JB. He's dead. Somebody got to him."

"No way. I'd have heard," Chris said.

"It's only just happened," Shelvey informed him.

"Who the hell would do that?" Chris was incredulous.

"I don't know. They've only just started working on it. I'll hear something soon enough."

"Just him? Anybody else?" Chris wondered.

"Just him I think," replied Shelvey.

Detective Shelvey reasoned that JB and Chris had never been close. Theirs was purely a business relationship, well more of a business arrangement actually. That thought was proved accurate when Chris said, "where does this leave us? Our arrangement I mean?"

"Nothing has changed as far as I can see," replied Shelvey.

"Well, it changes things for me," Chris put in. "I want more now."

"I agree. That's reasonable, so I think I can make it a third."

"Go to hell! I want half," Chris was agitated now.

"I can't do that. It's more risky for me now." Shelvey was not to be moved.

"Why? How can it be riskier?" asked Chris, folding his arms to show his determination.

"Think for a minute," said Shelvey. "There will be an investigation. Actually, it's already started. Some eager beaver might turn something up at JB's linking him to me. I'll have to buy a few more people off."

Chris was not convinced. "Rubbish. Nobody's looking at you or ever will."

Shelvey shrugged his shoulders. "Well, if you want to finish, you could always find yourself another officer to work with."

"Oh, sure. They grow on trees, don't they? Perhaps I'll look one up on the net, or the phonebook. Are they listed under any heading?" Chris was sulking now.

"Look, give it a few months and we'll see how things are. There's no point in spoiling a good thing, just for a bit of patience. Let things calm down and then I'll put it up a bit." Shelvey wasn't in the mood to give away too much, but was at the same time aware of the need to keep Chris in line and quiet.

"Ok." Chris conceded, "but I still want the Rolex."

"I'm sure that won't be a problem. He'll be only too glad to give us what we want and walk away." Shelvey smiled reassurance at Chris, who allowed a faint smile to cross his face.

They stood in silence for a few minutes and, right on time, the tourist with a guilty secret arrived. He face reflected hurt, anger and terror. Chris thought that a difficult look to achieve all at the same time.

"I've got it," he whispered. There was nothing in his hands, no case or bag, but money can be surprisingly well hidden at times. He produced a small envelope and meekly handed it to Shelvey. There was silence as Shelvey counted the cash, despite the tourist's assurance that it was all there.

"The watch as well, please," Shelvey could afford to be polite.

The tourist pulled a face, but handed it over because he knew he was in no position to argue. He was rewarded with the return of his driving licence. He didn't bother to enquire about the cash that had been taken from the room. He was just relieved to be able walk away in one piece.

Shelvey grinned. "Perhaps this isn't such a nice place to visit after all. I like living here though."

The two men divided the money and Chris slipped the Rolex onto his wrist. It didn't fit, but that didn't concern him.

"I'll get some links taken out," he said, smiling with pleasure at his new possession.

They decided to celebrate their achievement with a drink. As they walked along the street, blue-grey in the evening light of the moon, a passing car caught Chris's attention.

"That's nice," observed Shelvey.

"That's more than nice," Chris countered. "That's worth more than a hundred thousand pounds."

They wandered onwards in silence and Shelvey considered how a mere car could be worth so much.

"That reminds me," Chris began, "why didn't you want to join us in the car deal?"

"What deal was that?" asked Shelvey.

"The one JB told you about. He said you 'd turned him down."

"He never said anything to me about it."

"Idiot," Chris observed, shaking his head. "A few days ago a stranger walked into the pub. I'm going to meet him now. He's got connections in the motor trade. His people lift cars which have been confiscated by police and other authorities before they've been logged at the pound."

"That means nobody knows they exist," observed Shelvey. "Clever."

"Yes, I'm thinking about getting one for myself," Chris said. "He says that if I pay him, say twenty thousand, I'll end up with a car worth at least three times that. I thought you might be interested."

"Oh, I could be interested," Shelvey's interest had been prodded into life.

Shelvey had a nice enough vehicle, but it was getting old and would need money spending on it before long. He had always wanted to own a prestige car, but police pay did not support that ambition. He'd have to be careful, though. If he went too far and bought one that was too expensive, somebody would be suspicious about where the funds had come from.

"JB never said a word to me," Shelvey said. Whilst saying those words, he was thinking that he was more than satisfied that the said JB was making his way towards another place. He thought he knew which direction he was taking.

They walked back to the pub, which was, as usual, almost deserted. Chris looked around, but could not see the car salesman. They sat at the bar, clinked glasses and drank. Chris was telling the barman about JB's demise when Shelvey's phone rang.

"Hello," said Shelvey.

"This is Motson, from the Murder Squad. Have you heard about the JB killing?"

"Yes. What's the problem? Have you got any leads?" Shelvey lowered his head as his heart pounded. He listened very carefully.

"Not many, unfortunately," came the reply. "But we have heard something and we're hoping you can help us out," Motson said.

"If I can, obviously I will," Shelvey said.

"How well do you know the neighbourhood?" asked Motson.

"Quite well," said Shelvey.

"It looks like one of JB's men was running a scam. We think it could run into six figures. We're not sure if it had anything to do with his getting whacked, but we want to talk to him. His name's Chris. Do you know him?"

Shelvey glanced at Chris, who was a mere six feet away. He was deliberately vague when he gave his reply, "I don't know. What's the scam?"

"This Chris character was working with somebody from out of town. They came up with a clever plan involving selling a confiscated car. The problem is that there is no car. It's all a set up. Then, when it's time to deliver, they tell the poor buyer that the police had just raided them and he'd have to forget about his money, keep quiet and disappear for a while."

Shelvey looked at Chris as he held the phone with an angry, shaking hand. He spoke into the phone," I haven't seen him around for some time. Leave it with me. I'll make a few enquiries."

"Thank you," the Murder Squad man, Motson, said and ended the call.

Shelvey walked towards Chris, who was gradually drinking his way through his second pint. He lowered his head and whispered, "I've just had a call from my supplier. He's got a shipment that's just arrived. He's going to meet me in the alley in a few minutes. He'll give it to us at cost. Are you interested?"

"Of course I am," came the reply.

The men pushed through the back door. Shelvey made sure Chris went before him and reminded himself that after he had strangled the man, he would have to remember to take the rest of the bribe money out of his pocket. Oh, not forgetting the Rolex as well. After all, a man can't really have too many Rolex's can he?

-28-

Detective Shelvey was savouring his coffee. He was sitting in a metal chair, outside the coffee shop, enjoying a spot of people-watching. The chair itself was not too comfortable, but he felt at ease with himself.

"Hello there," a man's voice called.

Shelvey glanced at a man who was in the process of placing himself, without a by your leave, in a chair across the table. He was vaguely familiar and, even though the policeman didn't exactly recognise him, he was smiling a greeting.

"Yes, in answer to your question, that chair is vacant and you may sit there," Shelvey couldn't help the satisfaction of a moment's sarcasm.

"Thank you," his new companion replied. The sarcasm had either not registered or was being deliberately ignored.

Suddenly, the realisation hit him like iced water and he gasped. It was the fake Internal Affairs detective, and he had his right hand inside a paper bag. Shelvey assumed there was a weapon contained therein. He was frozen.

"Relax," the man said, laughing at his shocked and worried expression. He extricated his hand from the bag. To Shelvey's immense relief it was not holding a weapon. The man was holding an iced bun between his fingers. His eyes mocked Shelvey as he slowly took a bite. He didn't speak until the mouthful had been painstakingly and thoroughly chewed. He was mocking the detective. He dabbed his lips with a napkin and finished by cleaning his fingers of any evidence.

"I'm not who you think I am," he eventually announced.

"Then who the hell are you?" Shelvey demanded.

"You don't need to know my name. It's not relevant in this situation. All you need to know is that we have a business proposition for you."

Shelvey spotted it immediately. The man had said 'we.' He had a thousand questions, but was canny enough to know that he was about to be told the answers without having to ask.

The man looked up, turned around in his seat and waved. Turning back to Shelvey, he said, "I'd like to introduce you to some friends of mine."

A man and woman, carrying the obligatory coffee, walked towards them from inside the coffee shop. They had been awaiting their cue. Shelvey recognised the male newcomer in an instant as the tourist they had conned a few days earlier. The woman also seemed familiar, but he couldn't place her.

"Hello, Detective," the man said, with a smile that was as cold as the polar ice cap and eyes that fixed themselves upon Shelvey as though he was beneath contempt.

The woman's eyes also showed no sign of climate change. She was definitely not smiling, he noticed.

Shelvey's attention returned to the man with, as yet, no name.

"What do you want?" he asked. There was no need for pleasantries now.

"Oh, I think, I'll let these good people explain that," the man said.

His attention returned to his paper bag and he took out another iced bun. Ice seemed to have become a recurring theme. The man concentrated on his consumption as the newly arrived tourist cast his gaze upon Shelvey once more. He was no longer a timid, frightened and defeated tourist, last seen sitting next to Lola in a seedy guest house. The man facing Shelvey exuded a steely confidence and determination.

"The proposition, Detective, is as follows. Please listen carefully. There won't be an auction this time. It's non-negotiable."

Shelvey straightened in his seat. This was taking an ominous turn.

"You will remember, Detective, that a few months ago a young man was badly beaten by yourself, a man known as JB and another named Chris. Both associates of yours, I understand. That young man was the son of a friend of mine and he asked for my help. Apparently, this JB and Chris slipped drugs into the young man's pocket in a bar. You were then tipped off and he was arrested for possession with intent to supply. The three of you set him up, in other words. How am I doing so far?"

Shelvey shifted position, but said nothing. He was finding it difficult to meet the man's gaze.

"I see you can't even look at me," the man said. "That's the trouble with bullies. They can't take it when the tables are turned." He paused to allow the words to sink in.

"The story does not end there, though. It would be better if it did.   We could have come to a more amenable arrangement, I think. Apparently, you told the young man that he could be let off with a police drugs warning in return for a significant donation to your personal retirement fund.   It seems the young man objected to being conned and took a swing at you. He was dragged into an alley and the three of you beat him so badly that he will never walk again, and he's got permanent brain damage. He'll need personal care for the rest of his life, including care of the most intimate kind. Now that's not a pleasant memory for a person to have of a visit to your town, is it?" The man had asked another question and obviously required an answer.

"I don't know what you're...." Shelvey remembered the young man and recalled the bad beating.

"Now don't be impolite, Detective Shelvey," interposed the man with no name, who had just finished his second iced bun. "I've spent a good deal of time and effort getting to know all about you and your activities. Please, don't try to persuade us that I could have been doing something more useful with my life. We all know what's been going on, so let's be adult and get this over with."

The man indicated with his eyes that the tourist should continue.

"It has been decided that you are going to pay for what you did. We can't go to the police because we can't be sure how many are working with you. We therefore came up with an idea. We thought it was rather neat, actually. We decided to allow you three to do the work for us; you were going to double-cross each other."

"This is rubbish!" Shelvey began to rise from his seat.

"Shut up and listen," the woman hissed through clenched teeth and the man with no name favoured him with a threatening stare. The woman took up the story, laying out the details. She said they had set up a con at the pub in which the man with no name pretended to be a con artist selling stolen cars and their friend's son played a man who had been tricked out of his money.

This got Chris's attention and he talked his way into the scam.

Staring at Shelvey, she said, "we knew you liked expensive cars, so it made sense that Chris would try to set you up."

Her husband added, "the problem was we needed a large sum of money to provide you bunch with enough incentive to betray each other. At JB's bar there was a willing prostitute, who was used as bait for the extortion. I was pleased when you kept raising the bidding when you were blackmailing me. I wanted to get six figures into the equation."

The woman continued her tale. JB was the first target. The man with no name pretended to have been sent by JB to kill Shelvey so that he'd get all the money.

"You!" Shelvey whispered, staring at the wife. "You're the woman who screamed."

"Of course," she affirmed, all sweetness and light, enjoying herself as she resumed the explanation. "We needed to give you the chance to escape, knowing you'd go straight to JB's place and take care of him. Then Chris took you to the other pub where you would be introduced to the car dealer.

The man with no name wiped his mouth with a napkin once again, leaned forward, and, using a deeper voice, said, "Hello, this is Motson from the Murder Squad."

"Oh God!" exclaimed Shelvey. "You knew I'd take care of Chris too. It was all set up."

Yes," said the woman, "It was so easy. Two down. Now we only have the last one."

"What are you going to do?"

The tables had been turned. Shelvey had become the timid, frightened and defeated man.

"The young man you beat to within an inch of his life will never recover. He needs care for the rest of his life.

Shelvey, ever the policeman, shook his head. "I assume you've got evidence."

"Of course," the wife said, her eyes glinting now. "We had a man outside the bar for when you went after JB. The footage is quite good. No, it's better than that' It's crystal clear actually. The sequel is just as damning; in the alley where Chris met his maker. Oh, and for good measure, we also have the number plate of the vehicle that picked up his body. We managed to follow it and it seems there are a few people who won't be best pleased at being identified because of you."

The man with no name delivered the clinching finale.

"There are three copies of the footage, each resting peacefully in different legal offices with instructions that if anything happens to any one of us they'll be winging their way to the appropriate people."

"You're nothing but murderers yourselves," spat Shelvey. "You used me to kill people."

The man with no name laughed. "Now don't be so judgemental. Killing vermin like you doesn't bother me one iota."

Shelvey said, in a disgusted grumble, "what do you want?

"Ah, the time has come, I think," said the man with no name. "Let's see. Firstly, you've got a holiday home, two expensive cars and then...."

"I don't need a list! Shelvey shouted. "Just tell me the bottom line."

"Shame. I was beginning to enjoy myself. Alright, we want your entire worth. Also, I obviously want my money back and I want it next week. Oh, and you will pay my bills as well. Unfortunately, I'm quite expensive."

The man with no name concluded his business by polishing off the remnants of his third iced bun.

The tourist leaned forward and added, "I want my watch back too."

Detective Shelvey reluctantly removed the Rolex from his wrist and tossed it across the table. He was a beaten man. His shoulders slumped. His three coffee and cake companions, however, did not seem to want to leave. He gradually realised that they were still seated.

"Don't you want to know it all?" asked the man with no name.

"What do you mean? There can't be any more," replied Shelvey.

"Oh but there is," he was assured. "You see, we haven't been entirely honest with you. I do hope you'll forgive our little deceit." The man with no name paused to digest and relish Shelvey's discomfort.

"Now, let me enlighten you."

Detective Shelvey sensed movement somewhere behind him, but did not turn round. His attention was completely concentrated upon the man with no name.

"Firstly, my name is actually Motson, believe it or not. I do not work for the Murder Squad, however. I work for a friend of mine. Well, to be more accurate for two friends. You know one of them as Father Luke, but, as you also know his real name is Frank. An arrangement, at the highest level, was made for you to be released from prison, but the arrangement had strings attached. One was that I kept an eye on you. We knew you wouldn't be able to resist returning to your dreadful ways, so, unbeknown to you, we managed your situation. These good people sitting here with us also have names. Please meet Mr John Lomax and his good wife, Leanne. They are also friends of Father Luke, aka Frank."

The couple took their cue.

"Goodbye, Lomax said.

"We'd love to stay and talk, but we're going to do some sightseeing." Leanne paused and looked down at Shelvey. "I love it here. It's true what they say, you know. It really is a nice place to visit, but I wouldn't want to live here."

The couple walked away, hand in hand. They looked at each other and both were satisfied at having been able to play their part for their friend and guardian angel.

Motson said, "you know how I like introducing you to new people? This time, I'm afraid I can't do that."

Shelvey was confused.

"Hello, Quentin."

Legard looked up at the newcomer and saw Frank. He was unsure what to do.

"You remember I said I couldn't give you absolution because I am not actually an ordained priest? I now wish I could. I sincerely do."

Frank backed away from the scene in the same direction as Lomax and Leanne. He turned and called to them.

"Hey wait for me."

Legard was lost for words.

Motson broke the silence. "There's somebody else here, but I'm not sure you'll be pleased to see him again."

Legard was still watching the receding figures and the import of Motson's words were lost. The hand on his shoulder also took some time to register. It caused him no concern initially. He turned in his seat and was staggered to realise that the hand belonged to somebody he had last seen disappearing from a courtroom. He had also met him when he had clashed with his wife over some horse issue. He couldn't remember the exact details.

"Hello, again Quentin," Ray Quinn said amiably. "I'm very disappointed in you. I'm sure you are aware that we are all judged by the choices we make, and you've made yours. Are you familiar with the Dutch saying that trust arrives on foot, but leaves on horseback? I ask because I trusted you to change your ways and you have let me down. Worse than that, you've upset my wife. It's appropriate really when you consider that my wife's business is horses. I can't stand the things myself, but that's not the point now."

Quentin Legard looked up at the man. With fear in his heart and fright in his eyes, he recognised the voice as that belonging to the ex SAS man who had given evidence against him from behind a screen, and the face of the man who'd had a word with him about the issue with stabling Lisa Richards' horse. He had never been afraid of anything or anybody in his life, but he recognised the voice that spoke to him, and the words he heard next terrified him utterly.

"I need a word," said Ray Quinn.

The hand remained firmly on his shoulder and the eyes penetrated the very depths of his evil soul.

■ ■

#0030 - 250116 - C0 - 210/148/0 - PB - DID1337343